PRAISE FOR

# *Deep Breath*

"Rita Halász is the Elena Ferrante of Budapest, with a heartbreaking humor entirely her own. I loved this novel." —Jessi Jezewska Stevens, author of *Ghost Pains*

"Rita Halász's Vera is easy to like, because she is a fallible, searching soul who, while trying to escape her own addictions, also searches for the answer to the world's simplest and most complicated question: what can go wrong between two people who love each other?"

—*Könyves Magazin*

"Rita Halász has, in a literary sense, breathed deep, and in throwing herself into the deep with her protagonist, she has found everything: experience, disappointment, recognition, recollection, and most important, peace."

—*Népszava*

"For Vera, stepping out of a marriage is like coming back up from under water. One is taken into a fluid, uncertain medium that is as able to destroy a person as it can bring them new life. This water is also a symbol for the forces that reshape a person: whoever sinks beneath it will, if they succeed in bringing themselves back up, no longer be who they once were." —*Bárkaonline*

# Deep Breath

CATAPULT | NEW YORK

# Deep Breath

*A Novel*

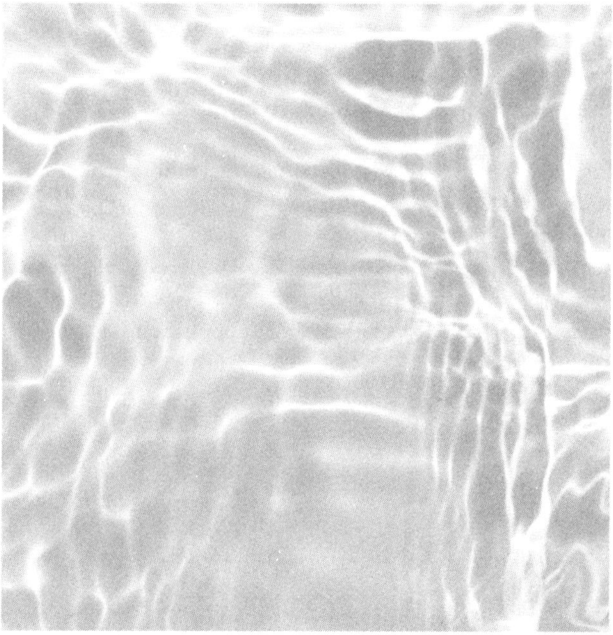

**Rita Halász**

*Translated from the Hungarian*
*by Kris Herbert*

DEEP BREATH

This is a work of fiction. All of the characters, organizations, and events portrayed in this novel are either products of the author's imagination or are used fictitiously.



First Catapult edition: 2025

ISBN: 978-1-64622-268-1

Library of Congress Control Number: 2024947759

*Jacket design by Farjana Yasmin*
*Jacket image © Graham Dean. All rights reserved 2024 / Bridgeman Images*
*Book design by Laura Berry*
*Water texture © Naoki Kim / Adobe Stock*

Catapult
New York, NY
books.catapult.co

Printed in the United States of America

10 9 8 7 6 5 4 3 2 1

# Deep Breath

I. Mom, tell us a story! I don't answer. I don't even say later, or that I'm not in the mood. My father is also silent. We move at a slow pace. I like how he drives, rhythmically, no unexpected movements. Andrássy Avenue is decked out with Christmas lights. And if the snow keeps coming down like this, we won't make it up the hill. Either the snow is falling, or it's snowing, only hicks say it's coming down, Péter's voice repeats in my head. There are boots on my feet. I don't remember putting them on. I glance over my shoulder. The kids are in winter coats, hats, scarves. What did I say about why we were going to their grandfather's? And why we took all our luggage? Maybe they never asked. They're shouting again. They want me to tell them a story, but I just stare out the window. The last time we had this much snow was in '87. We rode our sleds to school. There were only a few of us, they put all the classes together and we watched *Tom and Jerry* all day. Iván sat next to me. He doesn't remember that. For a moment, I thought to write him. I came, you can find me at my father's house. No, I shouldn't.

What kind of story are you looking for? my father asks. The one where spring chases off winter. Mom, tell us the story! Leave your mother alone. My father has hydronic heating, I might use the bathroom more often. The bathroom was freezing at our place on Izabella Street, so I'd just hold it. That's what I do best. Hold things in. I need to find work. I'll ask my friends, I'll write a résumé, a cover letter. For years, I've just been sitting at home, though all I've wanted is to be around other people, to feel useful again, I'm begging you to please hire me. I'm sure my father's house is a chaotic mess. And cold. But I shouldn't run my mouth, he doesn't handle it well if I complain. I'll ask him to turn up the heat. Tomorrow I'll start cleaning. We won't be too comfortable in my old room, but we should fit. The kids will sleep on the fold-out couch, and I'll sleep on the bed.

I haven't seen the city this white in a long time. Everything is soft, cars creep along slowly, people are calm. I fold down the mirror above my head and can't see anything on my face. It would be nice if things could stay this way. Spend all night in the car. I'd watch the snowy streets, Budapest all lit up. The kids would sleep. My father can't usually stay quiet for long, but this time he'd let us sit in silence. He wouldn't ask meaningless questions. He wouldn't ask anything at all.

We wind our way up the road. The neighbor is shoveling the snow in front of the house, he starts asking questions that my father answers for me. The snow in the yard must be at least a meter high, it lights up the darkness. I open the door to a familiar smell, a familiar sight, the brown bench at the entryway, my father's shoes sticking out the top. The thermostat is set to 18°C. You can turn it up if you want, my father says behind me. I'm glad I don't have to ask. We take several trips for our bags. I sit the kids in front of the TV, and my father and I agree that he'll cook dinner, and I'll unpack.

The cold surges from my old room. Piled on the floor are cloth bags, suitcases, plastic bags, boxes, and a rolled-up rug. So the garage must be full. I can't move the heater any closer. I sink into the chair and am unable to move. I look at the fold-out couch. Péter and I had such great sex here before the wedding.

The doorbell rings. My mother's here. A few years after she left my father, I also moved out. Péter and I got married, and here time stopped. She hugs me. I blubber on about how I shouldn't have come, the kindergarten is an hour away, I have no work and no money, and the apartment is sticky with grime. You're safe here, she answers. You just need to clean and straighten things up. But you can't straighten this up. That's just an illusion.

My mother and I stand stiff in front of the yellow ETA 2400 vacuum that they bought the year I was born. I already begged my father to buy a new one years ago because it hardly works. There's nothing wrong with it, you just have to change the filter. I've already put in a new filter, and it's still dirty. Yes, it might not work well, but it does work. We're too picky, that's our problem, case closed. My mother straightens up and fixes her hair. Endre, it's about time you get a new vacuum. The MediaMarkt is still open, I'll be right back. Come on, Babika, don't do this. You don't have to pay for it, my mother says. She pulls herself together and gets into the car.

All three of us lie on the fold-out couch and I wait for the kids to fall asleep so that I can move to my bed. The last time I slept here was with Péter. It was summer and we only used a sheet. I thought I'd be safe with him anywhere. Will we sleep here tomorrow? the older one whispers. Yes. She doesn't ask why, maybe she's afraid of the answer. I'm also afraid. Everything's different here, she continues, the walls are so small. What do you mean small? She's thinking about the height of the room. You don't like it? It was better at home.

The snow's still coming down, says the little one, and then the older one corrects her, the snow isn't coming down, it's falling. It's as if I'm listening to Péter. She has the same exacting tone. I never argued that you can say it either way, people do, it's grammatically correct. I just used his words. Anyway, falling really does sound prettier, more refined, I tried to convince myself, though I felt fake, it didn't sound like me. You can say coming down, I say to break the silence. But Dad says it's ugly. It's not really ugly, I say. Just different.

And what if my mother isn't right? That's what I wake up to at five thirty in the morning. We can fix it, we just have to want it. Just because she's divorced doesn't mean I have to give up after the first struggle. There's a layer of grayish snow on the window. I can't see out. The kids are asleep, my father promised he'd take them to the kindergarten this week. The little one's only been going for a few weeks, I didn't even react when she got the hanger emblem to stick on all her things. When they told me the older one would be a pail, I almost cried. I'd arrived late to the parents' meeting, all the good emblems had been claimed. Is there anything a little bit cuter, I asked. Just a pot. I kept the pail.

I have to vacuum and mop, but first, dust. Sometimes I forget the order of these things. Péter's right, I'm a wretched housewife. I hate that word. My father often said, Babika, we should sign you up for housewife lessons. You're so useless, goddammit, I should put you in housewife school. That's what Péter said to me. And maybe if I'd fought back, told him not to talk to me like that, I'd still be on Izabella Street, and he'd massage my feet or bring me tea and french toast in the morning. I imagine how I could yell. I could strike the mattress with my fists, pound my head against the pillow, bite at the sheets, but instead I just lie there motionless. On the shelf sits *Greek Tales and Legends*. I read it for the first time after the fifth grade. In the beginning there was Chaos, and then they list a thousand names explaining how the world was born. I didn't understand a thing. I read it again, but I still didn't get it. I took out a sheet of paper, wrote down the names, the events, I drew a family tree until it was clear what had happened. That's what I need now, just a pencil and some paper. No, a pen. Untangle all the threads, the reasons, the results, the arrows, the boxed-in words, the roman and arabic numerals. I don't crawl out of bed for paper because the floorboards might creak. At this time of morning, even the tiniest movement is dangerous. The kids wake up easily. I lie on my back with my eyes open. I don't even blink. I don't breathe. I'm silent so that I can think.

I scrub the corners of the bathroom with a toothbrush for half an hour. I've already cleaned it twice with Domestos and vinegar. Vinegar made Péter gag. My father took the kids to kindergarten this morning, calling from the doorway: maybe try not to throw everything out. Twenty-two dusty bottles that are either expired or empty. Shampoo, shower gel, deodorant, shaving cream, aftershave, jars of white pharmaceutical creams with dried yellow crusts. I pull my father's clothes from the drying rack. They smell. Dirtier around the collar and stained in several places. They need to be rewashed. He doesn't have stain remover, so I rub soap into the fabric. I open the lid to the washing machine and the handle is half-broken. It's a thirty-five-year-old Hajdu washing machine, the best, according to my father.

I go to the bathroom for the second time today, that's how much hydronic heating matters. Just now, I notice how clean it is. My mother came back after all these years to scrub the toilet clean. Andi writes that I should take a photo of my neck. I don't answer. I pace around the flat, enjoying how warm and bright it is, how good it is to be alone, and I look at the trees outside, the thick layer of snow on their branches. A clattering, snapping sound comes from the bathroom. The washing machine. I pull the plug from the outlet, the lid struggles to open. The washing drum is up too high. I can't turn it. It won't move at all. Did I close the lid wrong? I shut the clamp on the tumbler and pushed down the arm, and it clicked. I remember it clicked. My father will be furious. I call him, it's better if I prepare him for it. He's going to have to buy a new one. He's almost home, he'll take a look at it. I shouldn't stress myself out. I try not to stress. I wander around the apartment.

Boy is it hot in here, he says when he gets home, and he turns down the heat. He goes straight to the bathroom, pushes his thick body against the drum, there's a creak, a groan. It's a great little machine, I'm glad I don't have to buy a new one. You closed the latch wrong. He stands with his hands on his hips, observing the mirror, the shelves, deciphering what I've thrown out. I'm sure he'll mention the creams, and I'll answer that they expired ages ago, but he'll just wave his hand. You don't have to take those dates seriously. Look at how spick and span it is! It looks so much better, he cries. No critical remarks. His praise feels good.

On Izabella Street, we had separate sponges for the bedrooms and the living room, the kitchen and the bathroom. If I mixed them up, Péter took it the wrong way. I could have remembered which one was which, but I didn't want to. Back home we never had multiple sponges. Yes, that's because you didn't grow up in a normal household. What you call housekeeping is abysmal. Your mother—let's not joke—can't even cook. My mother's a good cook but she stays out of the kitchen if she can help it. Her homemade egg dumplings, for example, are unmatched. She mixes the dough to taste, scrapes the paste from the bowl onto the cutting board, then cuts it into long strips with a narrow icing spatula and dices them up. She covers the bottom of her frying pan, the big red one with the chipped porcelain coating, with the dumplings, then she cracks eight eggs, though she tells my father six. Babika, four would have been enough. She scrapes the dough from the bottom for me.

The washing machine stops, and my father notices with horror that I put his clothes in for another cycle. They smelled really bad, I say while I pull out a shirt and hold it under his nose. Now smell how fresh it is. It's still a waste, of water, of electricity, of money. I come with stains and the smell of wet dog. I wait for him to become agitated, to raise his voice. He sighs and says, fine, do it however you see fit.

I write a to-do list. Living room, kitchen, job search. Call Péter and ask him to put money into our joint account. I don't want to hear his voice. I go to the mirror and pull the scarf from my neck. You're crazy, nothing happened. A light red mark. What am I going to photograph? It's laughable, you can hardly see it anymore. It's not even red, more of a brown. The skin grew thicker where he dug in his nail.

For two hours I sit motionless on the couch. Outside the snow is coming down in large flakes. It's five o'clock, they'll be home soon from the kindergarten. I type Iván's number into my phone. I learned indirectly, when we were watching a movie together, that Péter would slit my throat if I cheated. I left, I'm at my father's, I write to Iván. I delete it. It doesn't matter that I'm determined to focus on only the good things, I still feel as if I'm watching everything through a black veil. I asked my mother if there was ever a sign at the very beginning that their relationship wouldn't work out. She said once my father wouldn't share his chocolate. Who breaks up over chocolate?

Last winter, Péter crossed at a red light with the little one while I stood with the older one at the curb. He shouted from the other side, come on, there's no one coming. I didn't move. You made a fool of me in front of the kids, he said once we'd reached the other end of the crosswalk. Authority tarnished. He's the head of the family, so if he says we can cross, we cross. He claimed it was a parent's job to teach their children how to cross safely at a red light. I protested. You're neurotic, he said.

My father brings the kids home. Who's going to be the first to tell me what happened at school today. They argue. All right, your younger sister goes first, why her, then your older sister, that's not fair, of course, because you love her more, you were more sorry for her when she hit her hand. I snap back at them. Was everything all right, I ask my father. He pulls me aside, lowers his voice. The little one threw a wooden block at a boy's forehead. It bled. My father spoke to the parents, thankfully the kid was the youngest of four, they didn't make a big deal of it.

They start to nag me, let's go outside and make a snowman! I don't want to move, I don't want to be with them. I want to be alone to think about where I messed up, feel sorry for myself, make other people feel sorry for me, cry, blow my nose, watch other people worry about me and then tell them I'm fine, don't worry. I want to go to cafés, to movie theaters, I want to read and watch strangers all day. I'll watch you from the window. You can wave at me whenever you want, I tell them. The little one likes this idea, she rushes outside. The older one stands in the doorway, wringing her gloves. Dad would have played with us. Her tone isn't bitter, just sad.

My father was right, that's what I wake up to at five thirty. There's a thick layer of snow outside the window. Amber light filters into the room. You both messed up, you were an idiot, and Péter was too. There are two players in every game. The fault's on both sides, fifty-fifty. Sometimes a little this or that slips into a marriage. Sometimes a slap comes out of an argument. But one slap is nothing. What matters is how he kicks you. It's different if you're standing face to face than if he kicks you off the bed. It hurts that he'd say there's room for these things. My father shouldn't make room. He should go over there and grab him, give him a piece of his mind. If you ever lay a hand on my daughter again, I'll slit your throat.

How did the vows go? I, Vera, swear before our living

God that I love Péter. I marry him out of love. I will be faithful to him, and he will be enough for me. I will be patient with his wrongdoings, I will suffer with him. Does with mean I have to be patient if he hurts me? Why do I have to be patient at all? And not in sickness, nor in health, nor in plenty, nor in sorrow, from life until death, I will never leave him. May God guide me thusly.

I swear before our living God that I will listen to the other person, and I won't just tell them to go to hell if they think differently than me. I swear that I won't just sweep problems under the rug, I'll handle them constructively. If my partner becomes angry, I won't hit them, I won't kick them off the bed, I won't strangle them.

I swear before our living God that I will stand up for myself in my marriage, I won't let myself be chided and hurt. If I don't like something, I'll say something, I won't just take all that shit like a martyr. May God guide me thusly. Amen.

No hitting, I tell the little one while I button her coat. Even if he doesn't give the block to you. There are other blocks to play with. We don't hit anyone. Ever. If you behave, you'll get a Kinder egg. The older one scrunches her eyebrows. She never hits anyone, and she still doesn't get anything, it's not fair. Okay, then you'll get a chocolate too. I wave to them from the window. Finally, I'm alone.

I throw out two empty bottles of detergent and a

torn, browned sponge. I'm not up to scrubbing. The storage room needs to be reorganized. This used to be my mother's office, which was once full of plants, with an enormous writing desk by the window and a bookshelf in the back. Now there are bags and boxes everywhere. A Commodore 64, planters stacked on top of each other, books. *Harvest Every Week: The Joy of Gardening!* For a while, my parents seriously believed they'd have a vegetable garden. There's a broken nightlight, five bags of clothing, picture frames of various sizes, perhaps from my grandmother. Four sludge-green pillows with yellow sunflowers, two suitcases full of tableware, fifteen boxes of thirty-five-millimeter slides. Yugoslavia in 1975, Paris in 1978, Visegrád with Juci and company. Bath towels, kitchen towels, and in another suitcase, stained pillowcases and five gas masks.

Are you sure we need five, I ask my father in the Skála-Coop. They're on sale, he answers, tossing the pack into the shopping cart. But there's only three of us. It's worth more this way, price-to-value ratio. You know this, sweetheart. Mom said to only buy what's on the list, I insist. If she knew there would be gas masks, she would have written that down too. Why do we need gas masks? Imagine how grateful you'll be in a chemical war. But who would attack us? You never know. And why would anyone attack us? Don't ask so many questions. Gas masks are important, every normal family has some. And is it a problem that we haven't had any before? He looks at the list, throws in a pack of toilet paper. Mom doesn't like that kind. It'll be fine.

We stop in the garage and my father opens the package, storing three of the masks on top of the surfboard, keeping one for himself, then pressing another into my hand. Come on, we'll play a joke on your mother. We stand in front of the door in our gas masks. My father looks like the bounty hunter from *Star Wars* who runs into Han Solo in Mos Eisley. Going somewhere, Solo? Yes, Greedo, as a matter of fact I was just going to see your boss. Tell Jabba that I've got his money. It's too late. You should have paid him when you had the chance. Jabba put a price on your head so large, every bounty hunter in the galaxy will be looking for you. I'm lucky I found you first. Yeah, but this time I've got the money. If you give it to me, I might forget I found you. I don't have it with me. Tell Jabba— My father whispers in my ear, ring the doorbell. My mother doesn't answer the door. Now my father rings the buzzer, longer, more determined. There's a soft I'm coming, then the patter of slippers, the key turns in the lock twice. Boo! My father's low voice booms in the stairwell, my mother screams and grabs her chest, I rip off my mask.

What's this nonsense? You'll end up dying in the chemical war. My mother doesn't react, just pulls things out of the shopping bag. I specifically asked you not to buy brown toilet paper. This will be fine, Babika. No, it won't. It's too flimsy. Aren't you being a little bit fussy? A few more words, and here it goes again. You'd buy everything at the corner store for twice the fucking price when the fridge is rotting and the winter clothes aren't even put away. From my room, I hear my mother crying. Could it be that she never talked back once?

I put the gas masks into another suitcase. There's an old microwave, a box full of board games, Police 07, Capitaly. Usually my father would win, he always ended up with Váci Street and Vörösmarty Square. All my mother needed was Kőbánya and Mester Street, where she was born and where she grew up. My favorite was Dorottya Street, my great-aunt's was Beszkárt. A strange word, like bumfuzzle or bamboozle, I always smiled whenever she said it. In the corner sit two bags of vinyls, *Thanks for the Happy Years*, Záray/Vámosi, and *I Only Remember the Good Things*, Pepita LPX 17507. A month wouldn't even be enough time to organize all this. I stare through the window at the white street. I need to tell my father they should be careful at the kindergarten, the icicles hanging from its eaves could be deadly. Péter calls. I don't answer. If I think of him, my stomach clenches. If I remember he's not here, I relax. I press my nose to the cold glass.

I met someone, I tell my mother. We're sitting in the car, just the two of us, heading from O.Z.O.R.A. to Csopak so we can watch the solar eclipse and celebrate my father's birthday. I slept four hours and I'm hungover, but I have to talk about him. What's he like? Handsome. But not like a pretty boy, so not insufferable. He's sort of—compact. Compact? Uh-huh. His name's Péter. Not Peti, not Petike. Péter, like a cornerstone. He has beautiful eyebrows, and his feet, my God, they are gorgeous. His body's all right too, even though he doesn't work out. The only thing I don't like is his hands, they're a little soft. But when he speaks it's like you can't say anything because everything he says is so interesting. You know who he reminds me of? Keanu Reeves, only he has lighter hair. Who? You don't know? God, Mom, you never saw *The Matrix*? It's the best movie ever. *The Devil's Advocate*? My mother shakes her head. *Little Buddha*? Why didn't you start with that!

He's twenty-two, so ideal. They haven't accepted him into the fine arts program yet, but they don't accept anyone on the first try, the yearly applications are thirteen times the enrollment, but if you're determined, you can get in on the fourth or fifth try. I'm curious to see what he paints, supposedly he's experimenting with psychedelic minimalism. I told him I'm trying to get into applied arts next year. He has a couple of friends there and he said he'd put us in touch. They traveled all of eastern Europe by train, can you imagine? Next year they'll do Italy and Spain, and I can go with them. You heard that, Mom? He's already talking about next year. I don't tell my mother that he forged the train tickets, no matter how laid back she is, it's better she doesn't know about that, or that he doesn't just smoke weed, he sometimes takes a little ecstasy, speed, shrooms. And you know what? He also works for theaters, and he designed the interior of a café on Ráday Street. He knows everyone, seriously, everyone. And Iván, she asks. She always manages to get straight to the point. I sigh. We met up at the Sziget Festival a few days ago, before the Faithless concert. I spotted him from far away because of the stupid way he walks. Andi and I had already downed two double wine and Cokes, so I pounced on him, and he froze, greeted us awkwardly, then introduced us to a tall, sporty girl. There won't be anything with Iván, I answer. I roll the window down lower. The light is strange, it's as if the outlines of the trees have become clearer, and the wind continuously trembles. When does the solar eclipse start? At 12:46 p.m., we still have a half hour. Your father wants to rent a paddleboat to watch the eclipse from the middle of the lake. He bought a case of beer, spare batteries, two rolls of film for the camera, and ten pairs of sunglasses, just in case. They're in the back. What does he need ten for? They were on sale.

My phone vibrates, it's Péter. Are you there? Yes. He's friendly, I give one-word answers. I don't like texting him, we misunderstand each other too easily. What should I say to that, to what, what you just asked, you mean what you asked me, what about you, you asked me what you should say, but you didn't say to me, to them, to whom. If we wrote each other longer messages, he'd use strange, convoluted sentences, as if he were trying to compose a treatise on theology. If I only read his messages, I find I don't love him. He writes that he put money into our joint account. He asks how we've been doing, wants to know if we went sledding. We didn't. But we made a snowman, I add quickly. We'll go sledding too. I promise. It unnerves me that I'm already trying to please him. He isn't doing well, his head's been hurting for days, he didn't go to work this week, he even went to see a doctor. He's afraid it's something serious. And what if he can't help that he's aggressive? The swelling's gotten worse and it's constantly overstimulating his brain, that's why he can't behave normally? I can't leave him in this state. He thanks me for talking to him. He writes that he doesn't want to hurt me anymore, he never did, he doesn't know how we got to this point. He asks to stay in contact, at least write to each other. I say goodbye.

My phone rings, it's the kindergarten. It must be the little one. She's shoved someone down the stairs, cracked their head open, stabbed them in the eye. Elvira néni's tone is clipped. Good morning, ma'am. My heart is pounding. Is there a problem? Chicken pox. I relax. It's just the older one for now, but she'd kindly ask that I bring the little one home too, she'll get it sooner or later. Her grandson just recovered, two hundred and thirty-five spots, he even got them on his willy, but he was a real champ. Hang in there, ma'am.

II. I'm cold. That's what I wake up to at seven in the morning. My nose is freezing, I duck under the covers. Mardi Gras is the day after tomorrow, there's no way I can bear it. Dear parents, we ask you to avoid violent costumes, Marvel characters, Star Wars characters, pirates, et cetera. The older one wants to be a mermaid, the little one a parrot. I'm going to talk them both out of it. Cat or dog. That's easy, you only have to make a tail and ears. We thank you for regularly supporting our class with cleaning supplies. We ask you not to bring any liquid soap, however we are out of napkins, and we are running low on toilet paper. We await your pledges for sweets and drinks. With thanks, Elvira néni. The cold is making me shiver, but I have no desire to get out of bed.

An email from Terike. Terike is Péter's godmother, a gray-haired woman who always has a smile in her eyes, as well as a grating, squeaky voice. After my mother-in-law passed away, she often looked after the kids. A short message, she's been thinking about us a lot, and at the end are three paragraphs about Saint Rita and an intercessory prayer. All I know about Saint Rita is that she was stung by wasps as an infant but did not cry. My grandmother always gave us a little booklet about our patron saint at Christmas, along with the year's horoscope. My cousins are Protestant and my mother leans toward Buddhism, so I'm the only one who read them. She's the patron saint of hopeless situations, Terike writes. Second paragraph, the patron saint of impossible situations. So, the situation is not only hopeless but impossible. In Spain, she's the patron saint of those suffering marital issues. She was born in Italy in 1381. It didn't matter that she wanted to be a nun, her parents had already betrothed her as a child to a rich man of a rather difficult temperament. Rita showed heroic patience. She acquiesced, trusting God to change her husband. Terike's instructions are clear.

Greetings, glorious Saint Rita. I kneel before you in strong faith, relying on your sympathy and love to help me in my great need. I pray that you intercede on my behalf so that I may have strength to bear life's hardships, and I ask you to protect me from every difficulty. Amen. Dear Rita, I am in trouble, please help.

I'm even colder now. I wrap the kids in a thick blanket. The little one opens her eyes. It's still early, I whisper, and stroke her hair. She turns onto her other side. I look at the thermostat, 16°C. My father must have turned it down again. I squeeze my hands into fists. It's what I do when I'd give anything to strike the kids. When they really get on my nerves, I lock myself in the bathroom and count to ten, then twenty. That's what Father Lajos advised me to do last year when I was still going to church. I confess to the Almighty God and to you, my spiritual father, that since my last confession I have committed the following sins. I wanted to hit my children. Grab their heads and shove them into the wall. Maybe that's not exactly how I said it. Either way, Father Lajos suggested that next time I should leave the room, go into the bathroom, and lock the door. I should imagine, in detail, what I would have done to them and how I would have felt afterward. At the end, I should thank my Heavenly Father that I locked myself in there.

The thermostat in the entryway says it's 21°C, but the radiators are cold. So my father didn't turn down the heat. He's sitting in the kitchen wrapped in a throw blanket, drinking his morning coffee. There's no heat? He shakes his head. Like an old dog who knows he's in trouble. I forgot to pay an earlier bill, they shut off the gas. When are they turning it back on? In a couple of days. I take a deep breath and say nothing, clench my hands into fists. Are we going sledding today? he asks. We already went twice last week. It snowed all night, the kids will be thrilled, we can go after breakfast. I'm not going. I'm cold. Then you're better off getting out and moving around, believe me! The costumes aren't ready. Are you in a bad mood, or what? I didn't get the job. Why, what did they say? Leave it. Come on, we'll get some fresh air, a little sledding, it'll be fun. I'm Skyping Andi this morning. Where is she living again, London? Lisbon. And how is she? Good. I leave the kitchen. I could be nicer to my father.

After breakfast, I wave at the kids from the living room, and they immediately make a fuss that I'm not going with them. I put on stockings, then sweatpants, a black turtleneck, a zippered jacket, and some thick socks. With tea in hand, I curl up on the couch. Andi calls. I want to talk about the job search, but I end up telling her about Terike and Saint Rita.

You're seriously thinking about changing the world *and* Péter? What, is that not a solution? I reply. Listen, Rita was married off at eleven and had her first child at twelve. Twelve. Her husband didn't just have a difficult temperament, he was a monster. He drank, gambled, raped women, and beat her. And it doesn't matter that he changed, his old enemies killed him. If you ask me, the poor woman must have been relieved. And here's the twist, really the most important part: Rita publicly refused a vendetta at his funeral. She wouldn't ask her sons to avenge him, even though that wasn't just normal for the time, it was expected. And that was her act of faith, not that she put up with being beaten for years.

Andi was five when her grandmother christened her in secret. Her parents wouldn't speak to the woman for a year afterward, and they wouldn't even let Andi near her. Then they calmed down. While Andi didn't exactly become religious, she often attended mass with her grandmother. Once she even went on a church retreat. Her grandmother was named Rita, that's why she knows so much about the saint, like, for example, that she wasn't stung by wasps, she was surrounded by bees, and they didn't sting her, they fed her honey.

Sorry, what did you say? I ask. That it's pretty wild to pray for the death of your own children so they won't avenge their father and go to hell. They died? That same year. Supposedly of natural causes, dysentery or something like that. I would say that's a little suspicious, but whatever. Her prayers were answered. And then once everyone died, parents, husband, children, she joined the monastery. She gets a stigma on her forehead, it gets infected, starts to smell, they separate her off, and she spends the rest of her life in her sickbed. Is that what God wants for you?

Listen, I start calmly. I was an idiot too. Selfish, stupid, careless. And? she asks sharply. You want to tell me that you deserved it? You weren't careful enough, that's why he was right to beat you? He didn't hit me. Okay, fine, he just tried to strangle you. I look at the curtains. They're lace, perhaps knitted by my grandmother. Or my great-grandmother. Or one of my grandfather's siblings? It could have even been one of my great-grandfather's siblings. I should wash them. It'll be quick, I'll pull back the couch, ladder, wash cycle, I'll hang them wet, I won't even have to iron them. The whole room will smell nice.

I talked to Péter, I say to break the silence. My voice quivers. He's been writing me every couple of days, and then he called me yesterday, or the day before. I answered. I felt like we'd cooled down enough. Actually maybe it was yesterday, I don't really know. It was completely normal. Wonderful, Andi says. I know what she's thinking, but I don't react. He asked about the kids, about the job search. He sent money. He's past that turbulent period, he wants to meet. What did you say? Only in public. Good thinking. He didn't argue, we'll do everything the way I want it. When are you going to meet him? Tonight. Where? Szimpla. Okay, but tell your dad to have his phone near him. And stay in public. Andi, calm down. Péter's not some wild beast, you don't have to demonize him! Andi sighs. You know, he apologized. Wonderful, what for? What do you mean what for? I answer. What did he apologize for? Well, everything. What do you mean, *everything*? Oh, come on, he apologized for everything. Well, it's easy to apologize for everything. He said—I start with strained calm—that he's sorry if he hurt me. Silence. If he hurt you? Because he's not sure he did? I'm sorry I hurt you, that's what he said, all right? He didn't say if. We're silent. If he apologizes for having threatened and choked you, then we can talk about forgiveness. You never liked him. That's not true. I remember, from the very beginning, you'd fight him no matter what he did. Did he strangle you or not? Andi's tone is hard, determined. But I cheated, I say.

After we hang up, I sit motionless for a long time. I think back to last year's class reunion. Please just come. That's what I'd thought in the bathtub. I shaved, read the kids a bedtime story, we prayed. Dear God, please don't let the children wake from the creaking floorboards so I can get out of here quickly. God heard my prayers, I was grateful. I said goodbye to Péter. Wow, you cleaned up nice. I had to tread carefully on the icy streets, I didn't want to fall. He wasn't there when I arrived. I was in a bad mood, Andi even asked me what was wrong. I'm tired. I have two, yes, they're very sweet. My husband is a huge help. Do you take them swimming? Do you buy soft-soled shoes? You have a beautiful family. Do you still draw? When are you having a third? The door opened, Iván walked in. He'd put on weight. We drank Unicum, he asked me how I was doing, I said everything's great, then we took another shot, how's married life, it's excellent, to which he said, you don't seem happy, and I said I am, we danced, he wrapped his arms around me, for years, I've been thinking of only you, he said, and I said, I'm not happy. He pushed me against the wall, he wanted to kiss me. I said no. Or at least, not here. I went home. Péter had fallen asleep in front of the TV, I didn't wake him. I wrapped the kids in blankets. Maybe there's still a way out, I thought. The next day he wrote. Let's meet.

The snow is coming down again. It's falling still sounds prettier. The snow is falling. The neighbors are building a snowman, they seem happy. Did we seem happy building snowmen? Did we even make one? Péter loves winter. And what would happen if I went back to him? We wouldn't touch each other, we'd just stroke the fat snowman. Everyone breaks up, we could start over. Maybe it would be better. I could love winter, I could love Péter again. I look at the clock, they'll be back from sledding soon, and they'll be hungry. I cook spaghetti with meatballs.

I'm washing up, atop the cupboard sits a large bouquet of Easter roses, the windows are open. Péter is sitting at the table, messing with his phone. I watch the clock on the wall for when I have to take the pasta off the stove. He doesn't like it if the noodles start to separate. They should be firm. The little one is crunching on her choco puffs in her high chair, gleefully pressing the gooey bits into her palm. The phone rings. Who's that, Péter asks. Andi. He grimaces. I put the phone to my ear and hold it with my shoulder. It's time, I take the pasta from the stove, grab the lid with an oven mitt, shake the pot a little, then I pour out the boiling water. He's insistent, I should hang up. It's important, I whisper. The little one works the paste into her hair. I'm listening to Andi, the hot steam hits my face, the lid slips off, and the pasta tumbles into the sink. Didn't I tell you to hang up the phone? Péter springs up from the table. He rips the phone from my hand. You see what you've done? He points to the sink. The big heap of pasta has a white sheen. It's nothing, I say to calm him down. I'll put it back in the pot and rinse it off, it'll be fine. You're an idiot. I don't respond, I don't want to make him angrier. I could have told Andi that I was busy, I would have paid better attention to the lid.

The phone rings again, and I reach across the table. It's Andi. I'm just going to tell her everything's okay, I tell Péter. He grabs my bicep, his hand burns. I don't give a fuck about your idiot friend, I've been waiting hours for that pasta. It'll only be a minute, I answer, and tear myself out of his grip. I go to the foyer, and he follows me, pushing me from behind. Get out, all right? Get out if you want to talk to her. He shoves me out onto the courtyard balcony. I try to calm Andi down. He's in a bad mood, this has never happened before, he's already apologized. The door is locked, I can't go back inside. I knock, I ring the buzzer, nothing. I keep ringing the doorbell. Through the window, I see Péter approach with his arms crossed, his expression crazed, like the boy in school who decapitated a fly with scissors. Please, let me in. I try to make a joke of it, he really couldn't want me to stand on the balcony all day. He turns his back and disappears. I want to call Iván. What would I tell him? My husband locked me out, let's go, leave your wife and kid, we'll escape to the end of the earth. I don't call him. I bang on the door, I shout, let me in. Péter approaches with a wide grin, holding the crying child in his arms. He opens the door, neither of us speak to each other. He doesn't apologize, but that night he gives me a piece of chocolate.

The kids like the spaghetti. Only my father comments that we had it last week. What should I wear tonight? I don't want to be too bold, too elegant, too attractive. I don't want to be pretty. Black turtleneck, black pants. Like I'm in mourning. Or a schoolgirl in a white sweater. I decide on jeans. My hair is greasy. I comb it, tie it in a ponytail.

Blaha. I've gone too far, I should have gotten off at Király Street. It's fine, I can be late. I stare at the snowflakes on my coat. They're shaped like coconut shavings.

I've never seen anything like it. Why should I trust him? It's happened twice, it'll happen a third time. I turn onto Kertész Street, Szimpla is packed, I climb the stairs, there's a bouquet of flowers on one of the tables, and Péter in a blue shirt. He's lost weight. It's odd seeing him again, like he's a stranger. I stare at the lines on his face. His cheeks are sunken, his eyes wild. He could really be sick. He hangs my coat on the rack, hands me the flowers, I thank him, then sit down quickly before he tries to give me a kiss. We drink beer. My legs are crossed, he rests his elbows on the table. It's good to see you, he says. I don't answer. I keep digging through my bag, my hands are shaking. What are you looking for, he asks. A tissue. I'll give you one, hold on. He turns toward his coat. I found it, thank you. I unfold it slowly, that also kills time. I have to be home by eight, I say. Eight? You can't be serious. My dad's going out to meet some friends tonight, I'll be with the kids. How are the little angels, are they enjoying the snowfall? Did he always sound so fake, and I just didn't realize it? Maybe it didn't bother me. Or maybe it was love. They're fine, I answer. I miss them. You can take them whenever you want. I'm not in the right state. He goes on about all the medical tests he's had done, how his head hurts, he wakes up nauseated, like he's going to vomit, he's so worn down. I hum in sympathy. At the neighboring table there's a group of Spaniards. Maybe coworkers. Or cousins who planned a reunion in Budapest. It's almost as if they all have the same lisp. Maybe they all see the same speech therapist. Or their kids share a kindergarten class, and that's how they've become good friends. One of the moms is having an affair with one of the dads. They're sitting on opposite ends of the table, at a marked distance, yet they keep glancing each other's way. The woman sometimes gets up to go to the bathroom, she's sending the guy erotic texts. Péter is still talking. I just can't concentrate, he says, I have to take time off work. It's almost as if my sight is failing. His face is smooth, all his gestures are soft, his fingernails trimmed to stubs. I think of how he leaned against the kitchen counter, a bicycle inner tube clenched in his fist, and he smacked the thick black rubber against the table at unpredictable intervals. Now he doesn't seem angry. Maybe he'll listen.

I sit up straighter and interrupt him. You haven't seen them in weeks. You could at least call every once in a while. I told them you were traveling and didn't have reception. He squeezes his hands, lowers his head. I wait for an acid remark, but he remains friendly. Vera, I'm going to take them, I promise you, I just need some time. I've realized a lot of the mistakes that we've made. That I've made, he corrects himself. Divorce seems to be in fashion nowadays, but we can fix this. He asks that we not talk about our wounds, nor bring up the bad. We should try to concentrate on the good things. Look at the shadows under his eyes. They're more than shadows, they're bags. Maybe he does have some kind of kidney problem, I think my mother once said that gives you bags under your eyes. Could I trust him enough to walk around the apartment without fearing that he'll throw something at me, or trip me from behind? When would I even want to kiss him, sleep next to him, travel with him to the end of the earth? I try to interrupt, but he's like a machine that's been switched on, he doesn't even take a breath, he just keeps talking about himself. He still has a beautiful smile.

I'll be right back, I say, and I step out to the washroom. I text Andi that everything's fine, don't worry. She sends a heart. She never sends hearts.

I return to my seat, Péter leans in. I want to ask you something, and I want you to answer honestly. I nod. Do you still love me? His gaze, his posture seem confident. I take a deep breath, I don't know what to say, I don't want to hurt him. Sorry, what? I ask to win some time. Do you miss me? I pick at the skin on my thumb, squeeze my mouth shut so I don't start laughing from nerves. I'm very scared, he says quietly. Why? Because you're taking so long to answer. I don't miss the bad things, I say, and I fiddle with the coaster. And the good things? The Spanish group has gone wild. Should they split the bill or pay separately, he only had two glasses of wine, why should he have to pay that much, last time they split it evenly, you didn't just have two glasses of wine, here, here's five thousand forints, and what about the mineral water? I don't speak Spanish, but this is how I imagine it. I have to go. Already? I told you I only had an hour. I stand, he helps me with my coat. That was so little time, and you didn't even tell me anything about yourself. No, I didn't, I answer. He grabs my hand, I pull back. It won't kill your father if you're a little late. He blocks my way. He's neither timid nor confident, he's squeezing the hand he strikes with. The bus only comes every half hour. But he could pick you up, couldn't he? He realizes I'm looking for an escape and he steps back, his expression gentle again. Will you go to mass tomorrow? I don't know. He takes the flowers out of the vase and rewraps them in the paper. It would be good if you all went. Uh-huh. There's a church nearby, you should go. It's important. Not just for the kids, but for you too. Or, even better, you could sled down there, that would be such a great experience for the kids. That's all we've been doing for weeks, I answer. You could at least give me a kiss, he says, and he carefully pulls me in. I cross my arms and don't move.

I don't look back, I hurry through the door with the flowers in my hand. The snow's still coming down. Actually, it's blizzarding, the wind is biting, it blows the hood from my head. I throw the flowers in the trash and board the tram. I didn't have to throw them away, I could have given them to somebody. Or I could have just left them on the bench at the stop.

He's losing his mind, Andi writes while I wait for the bus. He'll follow through with it, believe me. He'll become a fanatic and rave in church all day. It's interesting that none of this ever interested him before, and now he's going on about the sanctity of marriage. I'm going to throw up, seriously. Isn't he afraid he'll end up in hell? Let's talk tomorrow, I'm tired, I write. Sometimes Andi can be extreme and unfair. She's always slamming Péter to the point where I have to defend him. She's right, he didn't ask forgiveness in words, but he did bring flowers. It's not the same thing, but it is a good start. The whole thing has clearly done a number on him. He misses me. He might have just realized what he's done, and anyway, he's sick. Andi doesn't think he's sick, she thinks he's just manipulating me. Like when he told me he'd kill himself if I left him. He needs time, then he'll take care of the kids. My phone buzzes, a new message from Iván. I've been thinking about you all day, I shouldn't. I miss you. Sorry. I know it's not fair. My heart pounds fiercely. My hand grows warm, my face flushes.

Do you hate me now, or what? Andi asks on the bus. She's the new girl who joined our class a couple of months ago. When the teacher calls on her and she goes to the front of the classroom in her loose purple blouse, Iván drops his eraser and gets down on all fours to gaze at her breasts from the ground. The lower part of her breasts, to be exact. I once told her about it, but she just said it's not going to make her tuck in her shirt. Why do I hate you so much, I asked. Because Granny sat you next to me and not her. She waves at my friend who's cackling in the front row. I let out a long sigh. I'm sick of her anyway, she thinks she's some sort of princess. I have to do whatever she says, otherwise she won't be my friend anymore. Fuck that, that's emotional manipulation, Andi says. I must have looked confused because she started to explain that her mother's a psychologist and she'll be one too. A child psychologist. Every day, she writes down the things her parents don't understand. It'll be useful once she starts her clinical practice. Uh-uh, I answer. I'm not sure what she means by clinical practice. What do you want to be? she asks. I don't know yet, I lie. We sit in silence, listening to Granny explain normal human behavior to the boys. You've got great guys at this school, Andi tries. All of them were idiots at my last school. Do you like anyone? Of course not, I snap, and then I grimace for emphasis. I brought two sandwiches, do you want one? My mom always packs too much food, it's her obsession. She wants me to be a little plump girl, but I'd rather be thin like you. Instead, I'm like her. Round but well proportioned. Mine hates making sandwiches, I say, and I enjoy the bun wrapped in a little napkin. We're eating fried-egg sandwiches with goulash paste. The boys grow louder behind us, smirking and snickering. Andi elbows one of them. They're just doing this so we pay attention to them. Come on, let's turn our backs.

Iván is sitting in the middle in a stretched-out yellow shirt. He's telling a joke. His voice cracks, there are huge brown shadows under his eyes. When he laughs, two little dimples appear around his mouth, and the skin around his eyes wrinkles like a vizsla puppy's. The father fox says to the little fox: Son, today I am going to teach you how to fuck. Follow me and do as I do! They walk along the roof of the house, and the father fox slips off but clings to the eaves, and then naturally the little fox also slips off, and he also clings to the eaves. They hang there for a while, and then the little fox says: Dad, I'm only going to fuck for five more minutes, and then I'm going home! Andi and I laugh. My hands grow warm.

At camp, Granny assigns Andi and me to one tent, my friend and two irritating girls to the other. I'm not upset about it. Let's sneak out, I tell Andi after lights-out. She didn't think I'd be so brave. Why, what did you think? You seem like such a little good girl. Without shoes, in our thick socks, we creep along silently, like shadows. We peek at the guards through the rear entrance, and we're already sneaking our way back when Granny shrieks at us. I can't bring myself to speak, but Andi steps up. Smooth, like Obi-Wan Kenobi. You don't need to see his identification. These aren't the droids you're looking for. He can go about his business. Now scram, before I regret putting you girls in the same tent. How did you do that? I ask Andi once we make it back. Just admit to some tiny mistake as if you've done something terrible. Look guilty, please don't be mad, we ate some candy after lights-out. That way you distract them. You did something wrong, but you admitted it. That makes you trustworthy. After eating candy, you have to brush your teeth, otherwise you might get cavities. So, you are responsible and obedient. You promise that it will never happen again, that way it looks like you're trying. Look sweet and innocent. That's all.

We're lying on the mattress. It's a cold June night, we've each got two sweaters on. Andi, I whisper. What? I actually want to be a director. Of animated movies. That's really cool. I lie on my back, thinking of my friend, who I don't actually miss, of the bus, of Iván, how he laughs and says, hey, I'll have a little fuck. Andi, I whisper again. What? I like Iván. I listen to the trees' swishing and Andi's sighing. I know, she says. You like him too? I ask, and it pounds in my stomach. Chill, he's yours. I relax. The problem is, he doesn't like me. How do you know that? He's always looking at other girls' boobs. That's how guys are, they can't look anywhere else, they're too preoccupied with anything big and round. That's not what matters. Then what does? For example, he struck you out in the Ping-Pong match, no? So? So. That means he likes you. If he likes me, then why doesn't he just play like a normal person? I can tell that you don't have any older brothers. I have three, and they're all weird. The youngest of the three struck a girl out from a Ping-Pong match, and she glared at him, and it made him fall in love with her. So, he always strikes her out so she'll glare at him again. The other one fell in love with his classmate because he thought she swung on the swings in a sexy way. How can you swing in a sexy way? Don't ask. I'm just saying, you shouldn't worry, boobs aren't what matters. And the third one? He's a real dick. He only cares about boobs.

The bus takes off, I reread Iván's message. Should I answer? How would I answer. There's a joke, I write, about two foxes that are hanging from the eaves, and the punchline is that the fox won't fuck anymore. I delete it. Maybe it wasn't even a fox. Why would a fox be walking on the eaves? There's a joke, I write again, about an animal who's hanging from the eaves, and he says, I've fucked enough, I'm going home. Was it a cat or a fox? I miss you, he answers. Cat or fox? Why would a fox be climbing the roof of a house? he asks. That's how I remember you telling it. When will I see you again? I don't answer. Judit is gone all week. I don't answer. Andi told me what happened. I don't answer. Let's meet.

After the class reunion, I only told Father Lajos about the kiss, and with little detail, like a scene from a film set in the nineteenth century, where the protagonist touches the woman's face delicately, then kisses her on the mouth, and the woman lets him but pretends to be shocked. I made no mention of how we fell into each other drunk inside a telephone booth, how he reached between my legs and I came. I figured God knows the details anyway, so I gave Father Lajos more of a big-picture sense. He brought up two things, and both confirmed that I should not sleep with Iván, which was completely understandable, as he is, after all, a priest. He said that no matter what it would end badly. Because, and just think about it, if it happens and the sex isn't good, that's how he phrased it, then that entire childhood dream, that beautiful, unactualized romance, will end in disappointment. However, if the sex is good, then it will lead to new complications, because no matter how much I stressed that we were speaking of one single instance, he answered that, while he is a priest and he cannot speak from personal experience, he can say that if a person finds something to be good, they won't be satisfied with doing it just once. He asked me to plan something special with Péter. A romantic dinner, a movie, a walk, whatever. The point was that we do it together. For the penitential, I got the Come Holy Spirit instead of the Our Father or Hail Mary. I should pray to the Holy Spirit specifically. But I can't pray to the Holy Spirit, our relationship is irrelevant. Jesus loves me, God takes me into account, Mary understands me, but the Holy Spirit? It's as if it never even existed. Or I don't exist to it. It's unnecessarily elusive, without much development to its character, at least compared to the others, and unfortunately the dove can't help with that either. I never liked doves, their voices always made me nauseated, not to mention the way they turn their heads.

I'm reading job listings and Elvira néni's email. Dear parents, we thank you for your donations. The Mardi Gras celebration took place in a friendly and comfortable atmosphere. Someone was so kind as to give us frog napkins, which you can see in the photos here. We ask the person who donated them to inform us where you bought them. Andi calls, she spoke to a priest and asked him about the Catholic Church's official stance on physical abuse. According to the church, you're exonerated. You should still give them the opportunity to mend things, and you can forgive them, but you are not obligated to live with someone who hurt you. For better or for worse doesn't apply here. All I can squeak out is a well then. I didn't think they'd say that either, she continues. I thought they'd respond with the usual two players to every game sort of thing, once or twice is nothing, but it wasn't that way at all. Of course, divorce isn't simple. Because there's no such thing as a real divorce, but I think you know that. Yep, I say, none too convincingly. The whole what God has brought together cannot be torn apart or whatever. Then comes the obnoxious reasoning, a valid marriage cannot be undone, one must prove that it was invalid from the beginning. Invalid? For example, if there was no sex. At all? Yes. Or one of you is gay and you knew it at the time. Neither of them seem to work, I interject. It would also be okay if one side was not capable of sober judgment. Sober judgment? Yes, that's what they wrote. Like if one person had been high? I ask. Why, was he? He always was. But at the wedding? I'm silent for a while, thoughts flittering about my head. I'm just saying this so you know you don't have to be a martyr.

III. I have to concentrate. Perpendiculars and parallels, houses, streets, it's not complicated. I have every tool to get to my destination. Point A to point B, nothing special. I just have to trek through the space between them. At the next street, turn right, then the second on the left. It'll take five minutes. The snow is thick, maybe it'll be more like ten. We were at the zoo around this time last year. The trees were flowering, Péter mimicked the gorillas, the kids laughed. I texted Iván from the bathroom, said I missed him. An unfamiliar street name. I don't know where I am, I don't remember if I followed a curve or went straight. I look at my map, and I hear Péter's voice in my head. What's wrong with you, you dumbass. I was never good with directions. If Péter asked me to navigate, we always got lost. My father argued with my mother constantly about this. Babika, you have to tell me where to turn, that's the only thing I asked of you. An old woman with a dog. I ask her about the street I'm looking for, she's never heard of it. I'm sure Péter's there already and I'm the late one again. Andi would say I'm sabotaging couples therapy subconsciously. That's not true. I asked Péter to see a psychologist with me several times last summer. In your dreams. When I went by myself, he threatened that he wouldn't let me into the apartment ever again, and he'd take away the children. I turned around on the courtyard balcony. Now he's the one asking that we give it a try. Maybe he really has changed? I walk back to the bus station, then up to the first street, turn right, second on the left. I turned onto the wrong street at the very beginning, I didn't notice the tiny little road. That could happen to Péter too. I'm not a dumbass.

I ring the bell. Come in, straight to the back, a low female voice says through the intercom. Péter opens the door and helps me out of my coat. He looks better than before, his eyes don't have bags under them. He seems to be rather cheerful, he wants to give me a kiss. I quickly kneel and fiddle with my boots. Did you find your way here all right? he asks. Mm-hmm. I'm sure he's furious that I said mm-hmm. It's not mm-hmm, it's yes. Come here. He touches my back lightly, and I quicken my steps.

The room is pleasant, full of plants, big windows, outside everything is white. Two chairs, a couch. We exchange a few words about the cold, he asks how the kids are holding up. The therapists aren't here, I don't feel good about this. Why the hell am I here? I should never have agreed to this. Péter will win them over, he can be so charming. It's clear this is the shape he wants to shift into. I sit on one end of the couch, take out a book and pretend to read. He paces around, drumming his fingers. His shirt is new. It's been ironed carefully, it looks good on him. He was always more exact with the ironing than I was. They're ten minutes late. Is this some sort of experiment? To watch us from some secret room to see how we behave? What would they see? Two thin, unhappy people. Péter doesn't look unhappy. Nor happy. A little distracted maybe. His expression is unsettled.

A tall woman in a long skirt, a short bald man beside her. They could be in their fifties. They introduce themselves and bring us each a glass of water. On the table is a little basket full of Kleenex. I hope we won't need those, Péter laughs, and it seems forced. Let's hope not, the man says with a smile, and then looks at me. I feel as if, out of the four of us, I'm the only one allowed to cry.

We introduce ourselves. I focus on the main points, try to be composed. Péter is being complicated, going on tangents. Why don't they tell him to stop? The woman reminds me of someone. Either an actress or a singer. She has a sort of hippie look to her, but elegant. The man looks like Kojak at first glance, though maybe that's just because he's bald. What was Kojak's real name? Péter would know. It sounded Greek. Tavalos, Mavalos, something like that. My grandmother and I used to watch the show a lot. Tavalas? Péter's finally finished. The woman asks us to tell them the story of how we met. Péter starts, and I continue, O.Z.O.R.A. Festival, Solipse, sunrise, it feels good to say these words. Tell us about Péter's family and his childhood, the man says to me. You know, the family legends. It's like I'm in an oral exam. I know what I want to say, but I'm frozen. Why do I have to go first? I'm sure Péter will go on about me and my family, so I need to pull myself together. Péter's parents tried for years, I start slowly. My mother-in-law had several miscarriages. The doctors told her she wouldn't survive the next one. My mother-in-law, however, thought to let God decide. She didn't have a miscarriage, that was the first miracle. The second was that Péter was born at seven months, and he survived. My mother-in-law always said he was as thin as a slice of bread. Family legends. He snuck out of school and hid in the attic and ate a whole sheet of cream cake. He solved a famous math problem the same way Gauss had. He wanted to be an inventor. And how would you describe him now? What do you mean, I reply. How is he as a husband, as a father, and where does he find his place in this world, professionally speaking? Well, Péter, I start, and I don't know how to continue, nor why they're asking me first again. I hadn't noticed the piano in the corner. Which one of them can play? I glance at their hands. The man's fingers are fat, the woman's are long. Let's start with how he is as a father, the man says. I'm sure it's the woman. Every morning, she sits at the piano and plays a mournful tune by Chopin. He's a good father, I answer. I relax now that I've said it. That I was able to say it. He's spending a lot more time with the kids now. The woman raises her eyebrows, and I realize: she looks just like Diane Keaton. After we separated, they didn't see each other for a while, I explain. Péter wasn't in the right state of mind, and he was sick. The point is, things have changed. He plays with them, he takes them sledding, ice-skating. He loves winter sports and winter in general. He can stand the cold. I hate the cold. Winter is hard for me. I find sledding and making snowmen torture. I pause. Why did I just say torture? That was too much. I'm not supposed to talk about myself. If the kids are ever sick, he peels oranges for them, puts ice packs on their heads, airs out the room every hour. I can't stand it when they're sick. I know they can't help it, but I still get agitated, angry. Because everything gets thrown off. Like last time. I'd planned everything, job searching, interviews, returning books to the library, getting a new ID, going to the pool. And then the school called about chicken pox and I had to bring the kids home immediately. They each caught it separately, so we couldn't go out for a month. It was exhausting. I stop. It's good I didn't say loathsome. Péter fixes everything, and I'm not just talking about the sink or a clogged drain. He mends clothes. He's a good cook. He doesn't even use recipes, he just looks at what's in the fridge and throws something together. Sometimes I feel like I'm not a good mother. Why do you think that, the woman asks. She's not really Diane Keaton. She's more of a greyhound. With long fur and long ears, all droopy, almost like human hair. Maybe an Afghan hound. Actually, Diane Keaton is like an Afghan greyhound. Has anyone else ever noticed that? Péter and I used to always play this game when we were traveling. We'd watch the people on the train and try to decide who they looked like. Vera, can you tell me why you think that? I don't want to finish the sentence. I don't want to say that I wish I were somewhere else, far away from them, that I want to draw again and live according to my own schedule. I don't know, it's just a feeling, I say to close the matter. All right. What kind of relationship does your husband have to his work? I have to pay attention to my choice of words, I don't want to be unnecessarily hurtful. Péter doesn't like his work, I answer. I don't think he's found his place in the world. He's an artist, but he's working for a multinational corporation. He hates it. He hates Budapest too. But I love it. It's unfortunate that he hates what I like. Then again, I hate winter. But winter isn't a permanent thing. I take a deep breath. In the past, he was kind and relaxed.

Now he's hard. I take a fearful side glance. Sometimes he's actually rather aggressive, I add. Why did that change? the man asks. I don't know. Do you perhaps remember when that change happened? Maybe when my father-in-law passed away. Did you have a good relationship with your father? Yes, Péter answers. I must have had a strange expression, because the man asks me: do you see it differently? I clear my throat. I don't know, I think there are a lot of things they couldn't forgive each other for. My father-in-law wasn't happy that Péter became an artist. He had an explosive temper. Péter didn't want to become like him. But he still did, the woman says. I shrug. Yes. I don't know. It's as if I'm required to act this way, to talk this way, with these exact words. After your father-in-law died, your husband started working in a corporate office? Yes. When I was pregnant with our first kid. Here I stumble. Péter doesn't like when I use the word pregnant, because it's so much more than that. A child is God's gift. It's something a woman is expecting. I could have corrected myself to say we were expecting our first child, but instead I just say that I was pregnant with our first kid. I don't look at him, though I sense he wants to interrupt. And then both our lives changed, I continue quickly. And if I understood correctly, you're also an artist. Yes, but after we had our first kid, I basically had to give that up. Why? I didn't have time. You don't miss it? Right now the most important thing is that I get a stable job. And which of you is the better artist, the man asks with a wide grin. I'm terrified by that question. Or of the answer. I would have to say that I am. I try to think of how to say it diplomatically. That art isn't something you can measure, that Péter is a lot more progressive. Vera's better, but she would never say that, Péter says to break the silence. Could you please, in a few words, tell us about your wife's artistic pursuits? Vera went to school for applied arts, she got her degree in animation. I think she was the only person accepted on their first try. He looks at me. Okay, maybe not the only person, but that still means a lot. For example, it took me several tries to get into the fine arts program. She worked in a studio alongside school, she did keyframing. What does that mean? the woman asks. A keyframe illustrator, I answer. The animators draw the figure's movements, and I have to make sure the figures are consistent. If they have three strands of hair, then they need to have three everywhere. After that, I had to draw the different frames. I spent a lot of time hunched over a desk, but I loved it. That's how I learned animation. It's funny, they don't teach that in school. The truth is, Péter starts, the applied arts program was dominated by a different perspective at the time. Vera was the first one to bring fine arts into it. It's true, don't be shy about it. They invited her to a bunch of festivals, and she won too. Which one did you win? he asks.

Oberhausen? I shake my head. Annecy. Annecy, that's right. Vera has a sort of interesting mythical, or rather surreal perspective, and the French liked that. Do you like your wife's work? Usually, yes. Usually? Okay, I'd say I like some of it more, some of it less. Do you criticize each other? the man asks both of us. Yes, I answer firmly. Just a little, Péter laughs.

The woman turns toward me. Earlier you said Péter's father had an explosive temper. Did he ever hit Péter or his mother? No. You sound very sure of it, the man says. No, or not that you know of, the woman asks. He never harmed anyone. How are you so sure of it? I talked to his mother. Not long before she died. About what? Feminine things. Why it's so difficult with men, that sort of thing, I answer, and laugh. Did you complain about Péter? No. Okay, maybe I complained a little. That Péter was never around, he was always tense, he said nasty things. My mother-in-law said that the men in her family could have a stern voice, but they had a lot of love too. She almost divorced my father-in-law once, but she pulled through, and she didn't regret it. I asked her when she would have divorced him. At what point? And she answered: if my father-in-law ever laid a hand on her.

Now, let's listen to Péter. Could you tell us a little about your wife? Let's start with her childhood! I wonder what stories he'll tell. The one where I drank pálinka because my father mixed it up with a regular water bottle, or my mother's favorite, which he always tells the same way. And then I turn on the lamp, and the sweet little baby with her little rosy cheeks is sitting right in the middle of an enormous pile of shit. Péter is silent. The man nods encouragingly, and the woman raises her eyebrows with a kind look. Nothing comes to mind? A first love, a prank? Péter is still silent. Now the man asks. Favorite food, where she spent her summers, her symbol in kindergarten, you could say anything. We're sitting on opposite ends of the couch, far away from each other, and my husband is leaning on his elbows, staring at the therapists, looking calm, only he's bouncing his knee faster. He says nothing. No problem, let's talk about what kind of person your wife is! Péter leans forward, lowers his head, and suddenly straightens up. Vera is a very sensitive woman. I'd even say overly sensitive. She's disturbed by loud noises, her nerves can't handle them. She likes to exaggerate the bad. Can you give an example, the man asks. For example, someone accidentally bumps into her on the tram, and she's still upset about it a half hour later. He didn't bump into me, he pressed his dick against me, I jump in, but the woman asks me not to interrupt, I can react later. Vera handles stressful situations very poorly. If it was up to her, I'd already be dead. A wave of heat pours over me. We were in Cambodia, five weeks, a backpack, very little cash, like you're supposed to do. We go to see Angkor.

We're rattling up a rough dirt road for some four hundred kilometers on a catastrophe of a bus. And we didn't even have, ah, what do you call it, Vera, say it already. I don't answer. He has to describe it, and the man helps. Dramamine. There's no air-conditioning anywhere, the heat is awful, you can imagine. Trucks are coming the other way, throwing up an unimaginable cloud of dust, and I pull down the window so we don't suffocate. It gets stuck. A truck comes, the bus drops into a pothole, and the window, which isn't plexiglass, just regular glass, breaks. A forty-centimeter triangle gets stuck in my artery. Blood sprays everywhere, like in the movies. Vera just sits there. She just freezes, she doesn't move. Like someone patiently awaiting the other's death. I made my own tourniquet. Now, I'm not mad at her at all, she knows I wasn't mad at her, but I realized that she can't handle stressful situations. She either freezes or she overreacts. The woman nods and takes a deep breath, she wants to interrupt, but Péter continues. I was lying in the hospital for a week, and I had to have surgery on my hand. You can still see the scar. And what does my dear wife do? She pulls herself together and goes everywhere by herself, saying she isn't going to lounge around in the hospital all day. Lounge, that's exactly the word she used. Meanwhile I'm lying there with a stitched-up hand. The right one, no less. You can imagine. I can't even pull on a pair of pants with my left hand, I said it'd be nice if she helped. And what did she do? She just rolled her eyes. There, like she did just now.

If you had to say something positive about your wife, what would it be, the man asks. Vera's laid back. I like that. She hardly ever throws a fit about how I can't go here or there. She's done a lot with the kids, nursery rhymes, baby swim lessons. Sing-alongs, children's theaters, you name it. She's a good mother. Though she's pretty impatient. She wears out easily, often without reason. Let's stick to the positives, the woman interrupts. So just the good, Péter repeats, and he looks at me. Vera's a good person to travel with.

His legs are crossed, his gestures seem calm and earnest. Vera doesn't really take care of things. She doesn't like to cook or clean. Was that true when you first met her, the man asks. It was always that way. So at least she didn't pull the wool over you, the woman says with a smile. Maybe she didn't really make this clear, but as of late, she's completely removed herself from domestic life, exclaiming that she's had enough of housework. I'll add, I washed all the doorframes before Christmas, because they were unspeakably dirty, and I cleaned out the oven too. She can't even mend the kids' clothes, she just buys new ones. Food is always rotting away in the fridge, clean laundry hangs out for weeks. I'm not exaggerating. I could put it away, but I don't, on purpose, that way we can see how long she leaves it out.

Why did your marriage fall apart, the man asks Péter. First of all, it didn't fall apart, he answers. Vera decided, one moment to the next, that she was going to leave me. I think there were reasons that led up to it. There were, but they weren't as desperate as she makes them out to be. She hasn't said anything about that yet, the woman interrupts. Péter forces a smile. I know my wife. Jesus, Vera needed freedom, self-actualization. Her parents are divorced, and whoever has that as their example sees no other solution. That's the easiest way, isn't it? I'm not holding it against her. It's true, I've been more on edge lately. I've said things I shouldn't have, and I'll admit openly, I've hurt her a few times. But she overreacted. Look, the thing that bothered me the most is that our marriage is in shambles, and yet she's out partying with her friends. So then you do think your marriage fell apart? the man asks. Péter's mouth twitches. Yes, of course, it did at the very end. Can you talk more about that? Why it fell apart? My wife stepped out of our family's life, just like that, as I've already said. She'd come home late, and she was often drunk. Yes, drunk. It doesn't matter that she's looking at you with those big innocent eyes, you can clearly see that she came to bed wasted. I'm working my ass off, and she's out there partying. For a moment, I thought maybe she had someone else, but Vera's not like that. My stomach clenches. If I wanted to have a serious conversation, she'd just smile at me. You see? She just laughed. I wasn't laughing at you, I always do that when I'm nervous, I stammer. That's interesting, because I've known you for a while, and I've never noticed that. I don't know if you've been paying attention to your wife throughout this conversation, the man says to Péter. But she's been smiling practically the whole time, especially when we introduced ourselves. I'd already thought from the beginning that she wasn't doing it out of happiness, but rather because she was nervous.

Vera, could you tell us why you moved out? I straighten up and try not to smile. Because Péter— I stop. I don't know what word to use, if I should be factual or expressive. I start over. My husband abused me. Verbally and physically. Péter grabs his head and lets out a strange noise, waves his hand, I try not to look at him. I try to express everything carefully, I speak slowly and calmly. The first time it happened, I said that would be the last time, and if it happened again, I'd leave. So, if I want a divorce, I just have to hit you real hard, is that it? he asked me. I said, if you want a divorce, it would be enough to just say you want a divorce. A few days later, it happened a second time. And that's when I left. Listen, Péter leans forward, I know what this is. Right now, domestic abuse is in fashion, the oh-oh-oh, they hurt me, boo-hoo-hoo. Women can say whatever they want, but nobody ever pays attention to how passive-aggressive they are when they throw those words around. Yes, sometimes I spoke stronger than I should have, I'll admit it. But please, physical and verbal abuse? Those words are in vogue. Pretty soon a man won't be able to say anything to his wife. Vera is fundamentally oversensitive. I've said it. You can ask anyone. She cries a lot, she can't stand crowds, she gets panic attacks, thinks she's dying. God, she's like that. Péter, please, let your wife speak. She's already had her share of silence, the man says. Naturally, we take both of your hurts into account. Could you give us some examples of the verbal abuse, the woman asks. My husband told me that I was an idiot cretin animal. Stupid cunt, dickheaded fuck. I never said that! Péter, please, you know what we agreed to at the beginning. Try to phrase things differently, for example, I don't remember anything like that, or I remember it differently. But when she lies? You can see for yourselves that she's lying. It's true, I did call her an idiot, and I apologized for it, but dickheaded fuck? That's ridiculous. The woman turns to me. Please, continue. He said he should stuff my mouth with socks. He should give me a real beating, that would bring me back to my senses. Péter leans back, gives a strained nod, and tries to look the therapists in the eyes, as if I were sick, a crazy person, talking nothing but nonsense. He also said that if my nose were bleeding I wouldn't smile like that. He threatened to throw me out the window several times. Excuse me, may I use the restroom, Péter asks.

I sit alone on the couch. I stare blankly ahead of me,

and the man leans closer, lowers his voice. Does your husband have any kind of addiction? I'm so shocked by the question that I say without thinking, yes. Alcohol? Just weed. But it's not clear that he's an addict, I don't know. He smokes a lot. But not all the time. It doesn't make him aggressive. It actually makes him clean better. He's a little obsessive about that, everything has to be organized, but most importantly, clean. What about lovers? It's like my lungs are pressed together. I reply, do I have one? Your husband. The pressure releases. I don't know of any. Once I saw a scratch on his back. He said he didn't remember how it happened, but he was sure he did it. Did you believe him? Yes. Was I being naive? The man smiles. And do you have anyone? the woman asks. Me? Yes, you. Like right now? Yes. I glance over my shoulder. No, I answer. The woman looks me in the eyes. Does she believe me, I wonder. You've never had anyone else? I shake my head. If you've experienced so much humiliation, and so many other bad things, what stopped you from finding happiness elsewhere, and what's stopping you now? Finding happiness elsewhere, I repeat in my head. So one should find happiness. The man repeats the question, but before I can answer, the door opens and Péter enters. He sits on the far end of the couch, and I look at the clock. It must be over by now.

I watch his figure disappear. Why did I think he'd changed? Andi was right, his apology meant nothing. He didn't take it seriously, he just thought I was being hysterical and that if he did this to placate me, I would come back. Or maybe he really doesn't remember. Is that even possible? Who have I been living with? And who am I to have lived with him for so long? Iván's message: when are you coming over? I'm alone until Sunday. I look forward to seeing you. I ask my father if it's all right that I come home late. No worries, he'll be all right with the kids, I should go enjoy myself. I'm thankful he's so understanding.

You don't take taxis much? the man asks after I buckle my seat belt and we take off. I don't know, I answer. I guess not that often. You're just so rigid. Rigid, I answer. He nods. A thin, rigid woman. That's what the driver sees in me. I sat like that in the therapists' office too. Péter would never sit like that in a taxi. They wouldn't ask him if he took taxis much. I'm really just thinking out loud. Is there any point to that? I don't answer. You know, the problem with thinking, he continues, is that you eventually come to realize the bad things, and that just makes you sad. I am a sad and rigid woman. I don't want to alarm you, but you need to know that if there's ever an accident, or even just a small collision, you'll get hurt much worse if you sit rigid like that. Every part of me is tense, my shoulders are raised, my hands clenched, my legs squeezed together. I take a deep breath, lower my shoulders, relax the muscles in my back. I let my arms down and lean back.

IV. I shouldn't have met up with Iván. Now I have to wait again for him to text me. There's no point. Andi was right, it's just childhood nostalgia. For a year, he'd been asking. What do you want? For me to fuck you sometimes? That I leave Judit? Three kids? You'll leave Péter? Should we live together? I was silent. I didn't want to define things. I wanted freedom, for things to fall as they may. In truth, I was a coward. Now I was the one to ask. What do you want? To leave Judit? Live together? Three kids? Or you just miss sex? Now he doesn't want to define things.

It's 4:00 a.m., I haven't been able to sleep for the last forty minutes. I either toss and turn or flip over the pillow so that it'll be cool. We're celebrating the older one's birthday today. My mother's coming too. Ever since we moved in, she's come by every Sunday, and then my father goes out to play soccer. I need to sleep, otherwise I'll be tired and irritable. One shouldn't be tired and irritable on their child's birthday. I close my eyes. I try to let my body's weight sink into the mattress, to breathe in deep. My chest rises, but it gets stuck and I can't fill it with air. Once, my mom brought us home saying that we were going to relax. My father laughed at that, but in the end he lay on his back too, and he listened to my mother's voice with his eyes closed. There was a forest, and a meadow, the sun was shining, the stream chortling, and we had to lie there and make each part of our bodies grow heavy. My father started to snort like a boar. I laughed, and my mother, I believe, was hurt. Or at least, she didn't laugh. I try to take a deep breath, but I can't. Someone is sitting on my chest. Or pressing their palms against it. Four thirty. I stumble down the stairs, stretch, drink water, as if that might help. It's no better. I pour some pálinka, toss it back. It's my father's pálinka, which he ages in a barrel made from mulberry wood. He's quite proud of it, even made his own label. The snowmen are glowing in the yard. There's a mermaid and a dinosaur too. I lie back in bed, I picture the meadow, the forest. My limbs grow heavy.

I'm setting the table for lunch when the doorbell rings. The kids spring onto my mother's neck. Verácska, are you eating enough? You look so pale, my mother says when she comes farther into the house. These aren't really her own words. My grandmother used to always ask, first my mother, and then me: are you eating enough, you look so pale, you're so thin, so sickly, and sometimes my mother would snap back at her, leave me and my diet alone. When my grandmother died, my mother started to ask the same question, and whenever she does it we just look at each other and laugh. Now we don't laugh. You really do look pale, she says, and she hugs me. Is everything okay? I didn't sleep well, I answer. What do you guys have to say about this awful weather, she asks while she unbuttons her coat. At least the snow is pretty. Downtown there's such horrible slush! I'm all muddy, look! Look how pretty you are, my father tells her. She really does look good. Single? She nods meaningfully. It's better that way, she answers. My father was emphatic that my mother could have a second husband, that the man, whom for the longest time he would refer to only by his last name, would not bother him. It seems my mother decided it isn't time yet. Maybe it never will be.

Children, you know what I was thinking on the bus, my mother asks. My father interrupts, why didn't you drive? I didn't want to. Why? My mother straightens up. I'm going to a protest. A protest? My mother makes a deliberate, almost defensive gesture with her right hand. Let's not go into it, Endre. I know what you think. I'm going to a protest, and that's that. My father rolls his eyes. What were you thinking about on the bus? I ask. I was sitting on the bus, listening to a French group, but not old hits—she gives my father a meaningful look—we shouldn't give ourselves up to nostalgia, children, we have to become acquainted with new things, that's very important. Remember this! So, I was listening, paying attention to the lyrics, because I've started learning French. Did I tell you? Surely I told you. Bonjour mademoiselle, oh, voilà, que belle cette, what's that animal, a teddy bear? My mother turns to the little one. A mouse. Terrible. I can't see without my glasses. Endre, how are your eyes? Good, my father answers, and he goes out into the kitchen. Of course, everything is good for him. What's mouse in French, she asks me. I shrug. It has just now become clear to me that my mother has changed. When she was in this house, she was always somber and quiet. She was even quiet when she cried. Now she's loud, making broad gestures, like an actress. So, as I was saying, I'm sitting on the bus, it's cold, I'm fidgeting, listening to music, and then it suddenly struck me that, good heavens, what would happen if there was no spring this year? And what if an ice age were coming? I try to find the right word for my mother's demeanor. Dominant, forceful? What struck you? my father asks as he brings in the soup. That there won't be spring this year. There'll always be spring. Yes, Endre, for now, but what if there wasn't? Climate change, you know? Please, Babika, let's drop it, this is getting everyone worked up.

Endre, you're just like the skeptics in all those American dystopian movies. The world's already ended ages ago, and they're still sitting in front of the TV, saying it's nonsense. I never thought people like that existed. But no, I was wrong, that's Endre. My mother's presence is intense. Maybe that's the right word for it. What's a protest? You know, my dear, that I don't agree with what's going on in this country. And so I'm going to protest, so that other people can see that. If a lot of us come out, things will change. My father waves his hand dismissively. Grandpa, are you going to protest? Absolutely not. You don't want change? No. Everything's good enough for your grandfather. Even his eyes. He listens to old hits, and he's sure that spring will come. I, on the other hand, my mother hits her chest dramatically, as your grandmother do not accept that we must ruin everything. What are we ruining? Culture, my dears. Education, health care. Why are you salting it, my father asks. Because it's not salty enough. You didn't even taste it. I did taste it. You didn't taste it, I was looking right at you. I tasted it, Endre. It's delicious, but it's not salty enough for my taste, which of course does not take away from its deliciousness. You didn't taste it, you just salted it automatically. Why are you saying this right now? You always do this. I remember a similar argument that ended in my father standing up from his chair and shouting, Babika, I'm telling you, I'll set up a camera right here, and then you'll see that I'm right. The promised camera never appeared, though my mother really does often salt things without tasting them. The problem isn't that you salted it, it's that you didn't taste it, and then afterward you deny it. Should I get the hot sauce? I ask to change the subject. Bring it, my father answers, and my mother gives a meaningful nod. When I stand up, I become dizzy. I cling to the chair, tiny needles prick my forehead, I'm sweating. My mother notices. Is everything all right? I just stood up too fast, I answer. I go to the kitchen, and my father calls after me, can you grab a small plate for the bones? I look at my phone, Iván hasn't texted. It's possible that Judit came home early. It's happened before. Still, he could text. Or maybe he realized that it was a mistake to see each other, that none of it means anything. He could still text. Or I could text him. I don't.

Vera, why don't you guys come out to the protest? We could go together. Let's go, the older one shouts. Let's go, the little one mimics. We're not going anywhere. I'm not interested in politics, I say to my mother. That's sad. You guys could do something, but everyone just hides their tails between their legs. Babika, you've been brainwashed. Endre, do you hear what you just said? I don't agree with you, therefore I'm brainwashed. No one's brainwashed me. I read, I think. Remember, children! That's what's most important. Read everything, and ask a lot of questions! You can't live without questioning.

Do you want any rice? Just salad, thank you. I'm dieting. You have to live healthily. Eat lots of vegetables, eggs. You never used to eat eggs because of all the cholesterol, my father says. When was that? They've since disproved that. See, that's why I don't bother with any of that nonsense. I ate eggs then, and I eat eggs now. It'd be good for you to pay a little more attention. You've got a big belly. Papa's fat! Papa's fat! the little one shouts, and she strikes her plate with her spoon. Chubby, chubby. Do you get enough exercise, Endre? Babika, leave me alone. Is my mother flustered, or is she just dishing back what used to be thrown at her? It doesn't surprise me that your father won't protest, but why won't you, Vera? You can't say, as a responsible adult, that politics don't interest you. Indifference is the worst thing. So your father is better after all. Can you just drop it, Mom? Of course, I'll drop it. We don't have to discuss important things. She draws her hand across her mouth in a broad gesture, as if zipping her lips. The kids copy her. This meat is heavenly, my mom says. See, Endre, I tasted it first. I see, and you didn't even salt it afterward. Because it was well seasoned. The soup wasn't. To me, it was a little bland. Why can't I take a deep breath? Would it help if I pulled back my shoulders? Or if I stretched? My father slurps, I lose my appetite. No matter what, my mother finds a way to break the silence. You're still a great cook! Somebody has to be, if our daughter doesn't excel at it.

He winks at me. I don't want to say who he reminds me of. Maybe she doesn't excel at cooking, but your place has never been so clean and tidy. That's true, my father agrees. Not everyone has to cook. Life isn't about eating, nor talking about it. Only important things are worth talking about, my mother says to the kids. The rest is just empty chatter! Understood? Now, what should we talk about? Important things. That's right! Is my birthday important? the older one asks. Of course! That's the greatest miracle. That we're born onto this earth, in Budapest, and we live and eat Grandpa's delicious food, and then we die. Don't look at me like that, Vera. That's life, children. Whoever is born also dies. But that's too painful. That's why we chat about how well your grandpa cooks. My good cooking is very important, my father says, and he pats his own back. Yesterday I made a snow dinosaur. Is that important? My mother claps her hands. Why, of course! Creativity is very important. We babble on and on, but art never gives up, it always peeks out, breaks out, bursts forth! Your mother is a wonderfully creative person, although right now it doesn't show. Do you want any more salad? You see, she's trying to change the subject with salad. Thank you, my angel, while the salad is delicious, I don't want more. Instead, why don't you tell me how your new job is going? It's not too bad. I edit a website, post about exhibitions and all sorts of events. Now, Vera, I understand that after all that time sitting at home you'll take anything, but that's just not you. Website management. You're a creative soul, sweetheart, you need art to spread your wings. We should be glad she found a job, my father says. Are you still drawing? my mother asks. I don't have time. Children, tell your mother that she needs to make art! Mom, I'm right here, you don't need them to pass along the message. Vera, without art, you'll be unhappy, believe me. Why would she be unhappy? asks the older one. I'm not unhappy, I snap. My mother grabs more salad. We sit in silence. My hands are shaking. Trust me, if you hadn't given up, you wouldn't be here. Péter didn't have to go corporate either. He's talented, but impatient. He thinks success just comes to you. Mom, can you stop? I'll tell you one thing, and it's what I truly believe. A person's duty is to push forward. Yes, I know, your father's about to roll his eyes, but still, it's a crime to not give your all. My father senses he should steer the conversation. Now, we've still got something! he shouts. The cake, he whispers, so the children don't hear.

I should take a long, deep breath, fill my chest with measured, easy inhalations. It doesn't work. It's as if thick netting has stuck to my lungs. This reminds me of the times the whole family used to come together, my father says. I pick the half-melted candles from the cake. Mom's family, Zoli, the twins, pretty much everyone's scattered all over the world, the younger sister's family is in London, the twins I can never even keep track of, Zoli and Mom's family—he doesn't finish the sentence. My mother rubs his shoulder. I miss those times too, Endre. That's life, though. People split up, they move on, they die. Grandma, are you going to die? Yes, of course. Everyone dies. And I'm telling you now, I don't want a burial, don't waste your money on that. Just spread my ashes somewhere, you don't have to wear black, just be cheerful and laugh. Speak for yourself, Babika! I want a proper burial. Coffin, speech, violinist. There will be a lot of people and they'll all cry. Now, Endre! What are you now Endreing me about? You're right. I shouldn't. But what's wrong with being cremated? Mom, are you going to die? the older one asks. Yes, I answer, and I hug her. Then can I have your high-heeled shoes? Am I going to die? the little one asks. Everyone dies. She bursts out crying. Don't cry, Dad said we're going to heaven, and when we're there we can eat as much cotton candy and lollipops as we want, because Mom won't tell us not to. Her face brightens. Let's go to heaven now! My mother takes over. First your grandfather goes, then me. Why am I going first? Because, Endre, you're the oldest. But it doesn't matter, if it were up to me, I'd go first, I'm not attached to living on this earth. The body is prison anyway, children. Grandma can't go to heaven. Why not? Because she divorced Grandpa. Dad says she's going to hell because of it. Your dad said that? my mother asks, horrified. My stomach clenches. Your father is an idiot, I would love to say. But instead I just say, your father isn't right about everything. God would never send your grandmother to hell, believe me. God is such a, such a, I search for the right word, the children lean in. Such a cool guy.

Do you remember when? my parents ask. I nod, but I'm not listening. Thick webbing has stuck to my lungs, it's becoming harder and harder to breathe. I stand. Where are you going? I'm clearing the table. I'll wash the dishes. Mom, leave it. I stand by the window, trying to take deep breaths, it doesn't work. Short, ragged inhalations. I take out the pálinka. Their arguing filters into the room. Why, do you think things used to be better? They stole just the same then, and they steal now, and they'll keep stealing, but at least there's improvement, Endre, what world are you living in. I look at my phone. Iván hasn't written.

I'm sitting in the bathroom. While I pee, I use my finger to write Iván's name on the door. Now, it's not only the school's bathrooms that are covered with Iván's invisible name. I think about how if I keep writing his name, he might start to like me. The adults in the other room are arguing because my mother announced that she's voting for the Alliance of Free Democrats, to which my father grabbed his hair in his fists and said, God, you can't be like that. He never said like what exactly, because my mother interrupted: the kids can go into the other room to play. My cousins are playing Capitaly, but listening to the adults argue is more interesting, that's why I'm sitting on the toilet. I also like the Alliance of Free Democrats ads best. A little girl is playing "Für Elise" on the piano, but she's messing it up. Not D-F, A-F-D. A-F-D, the source of a pure voice. The boys always play the piano during passing period. Iván usually plays tunes from the intro to *Delta* and the Malév commercial interchangeably. My father will vote for the Hungarian Democratic Forum. Their placards say NO COMMIES, or something like that. The point is, the Russians are leaving. Supposedly we should be happy about that. I'm a little sad about it, because we can't be Pioneers anymore and I won't see Iván as often. Right now, we're in the same troop. He's the flag bearer, and I'm the campfire song leader. My grandmother is voting for the small farmers' party, even though the future is with the new generation. The small farmers' dwarves hold shovels in their hands. I wouldn't vote for them. On the Fidesz banner there's a young couple kissing. I've never kissed anyone, but I've often imagined what it would be like, and that's when I think of Iván. Fidesz is his favorite, because of Roxette. I hate Roxette. If I think of how Iván likes their music,

I instead try to picture his calves and his smile. I use my finger to write his name on the door twice more before I flush the toilet.

I go into the other room, and my mother's standing at the table with a plate of horseradish sauce in her hand. Just drop it about the Jews, she shouts. All I know about Jews is what my grandmother says at every opportunity, that they didn't let my grandfather into the university. He wanted to be a surgeon, and he applied four times, but they never accepted him because he was outside their class. I never understood that phrase. My grandfather was very smart, so I'm a little mad at the Jews. My mother would have liked to name me Judit, but according to my father, we don't give Jewish names to our children. Although he also said that if he ever had a son, he'd be fine with the name Dávid. I never had any siblings, and there's no one with a Jewish name in the family. My mother is nervous. It seems the situation is far more complicated than what my grandmother claims. My grandfather says nothing, he lowers his eyes. My father shushes my grandmother and praises the horseradish sauce.

In the evening, I ask my father who these Jews are. He sighs deeply. How do I explain it. The Jews, you know, they live in Israel. They're the chosen people. My mother steps into the room with a towel wrapped around her head. Jewish men are gorgeous. Babika, that's your fetish, you and your Jews. Endre, everyone thinks you're

Jewish. My father waves his hand. Leave me alone. I don't understand this Jew thing, no matter what I ask my father. However, I do understand that they aren't any good at soccer and this is a problem. Soccer is important, we always cheer. If my father's watching a soccer match, you aren't allowed to say anything. I would like to tell him that I finally got a 5 in math class, but he shushes me. He doesn't give a little shhh, he draws out the shhhhst. Then I sit down next to him and we watch the match together. You can talk about soccer, like, for example, if he thinks it was offside, or why they get a penalty kick. If Fradi's playing, we cheer them on. We don't support the MTK. Although I do, in secret, because that's Iván's favorite team. Was Jesus a Jew? I ask my father, to which his eyes grow wide. Of course, my mother says while brushing her hair. Jesus was a very handsome Jewish man. If Jesus was a Jew, that's good, right? It's not that simple, my father starts, to which my mother interrupts, of course it's that simple. And that little boy in your class—my mother turns to look at me—he is also such a beautiful Jewish boy! I don't know who she's talking about. I didn't even know I had a Jewish classmate. Iván! she shouts. I'm startled. My father grimaces. I have no problem with Jews, just don't find yourself a Jewish husband. My mother jumps up, always the *but,* and now they're arguing about the elections. Meanwhile I'm thinking about Iván. Vera, why aren't you saying anything? Sorry? I answer. My father and mother look at me curiously. I don't remember when I came back from the kitchen, but it appears I did, because I'm sitting at the table. I think about what would happen if I were never able to breathe again. Did I have one or two shots of pálinka? Can they smell it on my breath?

I ask the kids which yogurt they want, peach or raspberry. To which my father says, why are you asking them, you just hand them one and they eat what they get. If they don't like it, too bad. Endre, why does it bother you that they get to choose? Because it's an idiotic trend that children choose everything. Should we ask them if they want to go to kindergarten? Dad, where is this coming from? Kindergarten isn't a question of choice, yogurt is. Now that I don't agree with. My mother sighs and runs her fingers through her hair. You could use a little freshening up, Endre. I'll bring you to the protest, at least you'll hear something different. I don't agree, that's all there is to it. Or can I not state my opinion? You can state it, but prove it. That's so liberal, my father whines. Now, there, my mother says with a slap on the table. He can say it's liberal. Yes, and you've already corrupted your daughter with it. Of course, I'm at fault for everything. You guys, don't start this! Your mother's always been like this. She always needs something new. Once she decided that she'd be a wandering gypsy and go to the Himalayas to become a Sherpa. This went on for months. Monastery, Tibetan order, Rose Calvary. Rose Cross, my mother corrects. Rose Cross, my father says, drawing out the *o* in Rose. Which yogurt do you want? I want the peach one, the little one shouts. Not I want, I'd like, I correct. Eat this, my father says. It's just as good, and he shoves the raspberry one into her hands. I want peach, she says, tossing the raspberry. I chide her. Don't throw it, say please, nicely. My voice is becoming shakier. I want it! Give it! The peach is mine! My father's right, it would be much simpler to say here's raspberry, shut up and eat it. My father is watching militantly. I need to show him that I have control over the situation. I want peach, the little one shouts. Sorry, I couldn't hear that, I say with a sympathetic look. Her eyes grow wide. I don't hear the magic word. What's the magic word? Please, the older one cuts in. Please, the little one whimpers. I relax. Endre, why don't you trust Vera? She's a good mother.

The kids go upstairs to play. It's important that they learn how to resist, I explain to my father, and he comes back with a *they're going to start walking all over you.* And anyway, what makes you so sure that your way of raising kids is better than mine? You were never so picky about everything, you ate what we gave you, you didn't interrupt when adults were speaking, and you didn't argue. Of course, because you beat me when I was two years old. After that you didn't have much to worry about. My mother grabs my arm. Vera! That didn't happen, did it? If I didn't behave the way he expected, he raised his voice. I had to be thankful for gifts, otherwise he would take it personally. I don't want that. I'd rather have my children refuse than be afraid. I wouldn't be here if you had been interested in what I thought. And that includes you too, Mom! If you two had taught me how to stand up for myself, to fight for myself, how to say no, maybe Péter wouldn't have—I stop. I don't know how else to say it. Péter wouldn't have abused me. But the only thing I learned was how to shut up, because I was only good when I shut my mouth. Don't be surprised that Mom left you, you criticize everything, interrupt everything, and Mom, why the fuck did you let it go on for so long? Jesus, right now you're picking at everything. So should we ask, Endre, does it matter how I hold this fucking broom?

My mother starts crying, my father stands up, telling me sternly, don't talk to your mother that way. Now finish your hissy fit. I'm not finished! I'm tired of you all treating me like I'm an idiot. I'm an adult, I can choose what's right for my kids. Vera, calm down! Leave me the fuck alone, or did you not understand? Leave me alone! I shout at the top of my lungs. My mother tries to put an arm around me, I push her away. Get out of here and leave me alone! I'm sweating, my heart is pounding. I should stop shouting, what are the kids going to think, I breathe in, always in, my lungs fill, in, in, in, there's no way out, I can't breathe out. I need to breathe out, I can hardly get any air, I'm dizzy, I hold on to the chair, I sway, there are shivers in my entire body. I can't breathe! Vera! Breathe! My mother's voice. Breathe, Vera! Andi's voice. Just breathe out! Péter's voice. I'm tired, my legs give out. My friend isn't well, give her some space. Andi's voice. Is anyone here a doctor? Does anyone have water? Stay with us, Vera, breathe! My wife isn't well. Péter's voice. Relax, you're not going to die, I'm here. Andi's voice. What's the matter? She just found out her parents are getting divorced. Your wife? We're getting married next week. Is she diabetic? She can't stand crowds. I'm crying, the cold is making me shiver. Someone grabs me. Endre, bring me some water! Should we call an ambulance? What's wrong with Mom? Everything's fine, children. Is she going to die? She is not going to die. Come on, let's go out to the yard, your mother's tired and needs some sleep.

It's dark. The streetlights are illuminating the snowflakes. Like magic. I'm lying in my father's bed. I turn on the light. It's 8:03 p.m. Are you feeling better? I turn toward the voice. I nod. You didn't go to the protest? She shakes her head. I'm ashamed of myself. It's fine. Is Dad really worked up about it? I told him you were right. I'm guessing he doesn't see it that way. He knows it, but he doesn't like to admit it. She brushes her hand across my forehead. Something like this happened six months ago.

Drink some water. When Péter told me he didn't love me. That he'd fallen out of love a long time ago. And then he took it back, said he wasn't thinking about it seriously, it was just that there was a nihilism radiating off me, and he wanted to know if he was still capable of causing me pain. I let her stroke my hand. Your father said something about you two going to couples therapy. You never told me. What's going to happen now? I don't know. What do you want to happen? I don't know. Divorce. I'm just afraid. That I'll regret it. That ten years later I'll think it was the worst mistake I made in my entire life. If that's the case, then you'll have time to deal with it. You could tell yourself that, given the situation, it seemed like the best solution. And you can even say it was a mistake. You can make mistakes. But for now you have to get stronger, love. Divorce is a real pain. People do a lot of stupid things, it's easy to become an addict. Why do you say that? Your father said you're laying into the pálinka. There's like thirty liters. He shouldn't be worried, I'm not going to drink it all. It's not the pálinka he's worried about, it's you. It was only a few times. I couldn't sleep, and it seemed like a good idea. I can't breathe properly, I keep trying to fill my lungs but it's like someone is constantly sitting on my chest. Or I'm in a tight corset. And this afternoon? I don't answer. Pálinka isn't a solution. Go swimming, it'll do you good. Water is the best medicine.

The door opens, and the kids rush in. I hug them. Mom, I don't want your high heels, just please don't die. The little one holds up a drawing. Is it pretty? It's very pretty. It's you and Dad and Grandma and Grandpa holding cotton candy. That's a dinosaur. Everyone's in heaven.

V. Far out in the ocean, the water was the bluest of blues, almost like the petals of a cornflower, and it was as clear as the cleanest glass. Down there, in the deep deep depths, there lived a sea people. That's how the fairy tale starts. The children listen without a word, they're grateful that I'm finally reading to them. Lately, I haven't had the patience. We sit on the bed wrapped in a thick comforter. The little one is leaning against my arm, the older one is sucking her thumb. I tell her not to, but she doesn't stop. I don't push, the psychologist said that for the next six months, every reaction can be considered normal. There were six of them, and some of them were very beautiful, but the youngest was the most beautiful of them all. Her face was so clean and so smooth, like a little rose petal, and her eyes were as blue as the depths of the ocean, but she had no legs. Like all the rest, her body ended in the tail of a fish. Mom, are we beautiful, the little one asks. Very beautiful. Both of us? Of course. But am I more beautiful? Because in all the fairy tales the youngest is always the prettiest. Fairy tales are different. So then I'm the prettiest? the older one asks. It doesn't matter at all who's prettier, I answer. I go on for a while about the importance of inner beauty, but eventually they shout that I should just finish the story.

The very youngest was a special child, she was quiet and reflective. I wonder what my father would say about how I was. Adequate. Adequate means that I was raised well and I wasn't foolish. Pretty, but nothing special. So and thus, I would only prove to become what my father had expected. I'm not being fair to him. I would also like not to have much trouble with the kids. They should be good, but prepared for life, they should be smart, strong, but not aggressive. They should be brave. I shouldn't be ashamed of them. Do I actually take a genuine interest in them? Or do I just shove myself down their throats? Myself and my father. Péter, my mother. Andi. Terike. No, not Terike.

The smallest princess of the sea was happiest when people told her about the human world. She would interrogate her grandmother, the old queen, about everything she could possibly know of big ships, cities on land, people and animals. Where's her mom? the older one asks. She died, I answer. Hers too? Why, who else? Snow

White's, she answers sharply. You're right, her mother died too. What the little princess liked best about the land up above was that the flowers smelled nice and the forests were green. And Cinderella's too. Yes, hers too. Once you reach your fifteenth year, said the old queen, you can rise up from the sea, sit on the rocks, and gaze at the big ships in the moonlight as they sail away from you. Mom, Belle's too. I can't read you the story if you guys keep interrupting me. Why don't they have mothers? Because it's more interesting that way. Why don't their fathers die instead? Because if their mothers were still alive, there wouldn't be any evil stepmothers who try to chase off the poor princesses and work them to death. Mothers protect children from a lot of bad things. They nod. Each of the siblings were a few years apart, and indeed, the youngest little princess would have to wait five years for her turn. Red Riding Hood had a mother, but the wolf ate her. Red Riding Hood's mother might have been careless. Did she have a father? I don't know. He died? Maybe. Or he just traveled far away. Or they got divorced, the older one chimes in.

In the evening, when the sisters wrapped their arms around each other and swam up to the surface, the youngest princess stayed by herself in the great big room, watching them with a broken heart. She would have cried, but mermaids can't cry, because the water immediately washes away their tears, and that just makes their suffering more painful. Mom, why did you make that sound? Poor thing. Why? Because she can't cry. Can we cry underwater? This Andersen is cruel. He could have written that they cry grains of sand, or salt. Or that bubbles come out of their eyes. Mom, can we cry underwater? Poor mermaids. Mom, answer me! I've never tried it before, I answer. It was already late at night, but the little mermaid couldn't stop watching the ship swimming in the light, nor looking at the handsome prince. Mom, why'd you say of course? Because it's irritating. She sees him on the boat, then poof, she falls in love with him, just because he's handsome. This is where the problems start. But you fell in love with Dad at first sight. Tell us the story! Another time. At that very moment, the ship's deck split in two, and she saw the prince drop into the sea. Please, Mom! This is the most exciting part. You guys don't want to hear what happens to the prince? He's going to survive anyway. Tell us the story! I don't want to, but they're so skilled at begging that eventually I start. Once upon a time, there was a girl. A very pretty girl, the little one interrupted. Yes, a very pretty girl and a very pretty boy. They didn't know each other because they lived on opposite ends of the city. And they went to different schools. Yes, different schools. And the boy was older than her. Yes, but will you let me tell it? So, they didn't know each other, but they both liked music, and they liked dancing, so when they heard that there would be a huge party, they were determined to go. And tell us about how the girl didn't want to go because she was sad. Fine, so, the girl was sitting at home, not wanting to do anything, because the boy she liked, I look up, didn't care about her one bit, the older one shouts. That's right, he chose a sporty girl over her. And so, her friend told her: it's time, stop your whining and come to this party with me. What's a party to me, the girl scoffed, I'm going to be sad for the rest of my life. Then you're not all there, her friend said, and the girl saw that she was right. And so, on a hot summer day, the girls arrived at O.Z.O.R.A., where music played night and day, and night and day she danced. She didn't sleep? Sometimes she slept. Did she eat? Of course, she ate, drank, and even peed sometimes, but if you guys keep interrupting, I can't tell the story. So, the girl was dancing and listening to music like everyone around her. And then, as the sun set in its pink light, she spotted a beautiful boy. And she thought, man, wouldn't it be nice to get to know him. The boy felt the same. They smiled at each other, they danced, they talked, and they watched the sunrise. Having fallen in love, the boy asked for the girl's hand, and they had a great big wedding. The End. Mom, are you in love with Dad? No. But you love him? I'm mad at him right now. But you still love him, right? I try to distract them, I clap my hands, we have the Mother's Day ceremony tomorrow, and we all need to get our sleep. Why did Grandma and Grandpa get a divorce? Because they fought a lot. Are you guys going to get a divorce too? Maybe. Robi's parents got divorced, but Robi's really bad, he never puts his toys away. Dear Father, our Lord Jesus and Savior. Keep me safe throughout the night, and wake me with the morning's light. And please bring us all back to Dad. Amen. Mom, you didn't say amen.

I close my eyes, and I'm standing with Péter in front of the church, a bouquet of flowers in my hands. I looked resolute and hopeful. I remember thinking I could step into this marriage with a clear conscience. Péter's face was tired, pained. He came home at dawn, completely baked. I didn't say anything. One shouldn't say something right before one's wedding. It would be like breaking a contract. I tricked him. I pretended I was silent. That was my mistake. And he wanted to believe it. That was his. Mom, don't be late tomorrow. I'm not usually late, I answer. She remembers the last Mother's Day ceremony, how all the mothers were there but I wasn't. I assure her that I won't be late. Mom, do mermaids pee? I pretend I'm asleep.

I straighten my goggles, look at the blue pool, everything goes quiet. I take a breath and try to exhale beneath the water. One, two, I stop, cling to the pool's edge. Tilt your head down lower so you can actually get under the water. It's easier that way, less resistance. Try to be more relaxed. Someone should teach me already what it means to be relaxed. I tilt my head down lower, count to three, exhale. I stutter again, grab the pool's edge and wheeze. Don't hold it in, you have to let it go. Think about it: if you don't breathe out, you can't breathe in again. My mother always says that swimming is the best medicine. Your back hurts, you're frustrated, you left your man, so swim. After the last panic attack, she bought me a ten-visit pool pass. When I complained that I couldn't swim freestyle, she paid for a personal trainer too. I can't do it, I say angrily after the second try. Maybe the problem is that you breathe in too much air, and then you can't breathe it all out. I can't breathe in too much air because a black incubus has wound my chest in a thick web, then sat down, and has crouched there ever since. All I say is that I don't think that's the problem. Again. Breathe in, head underwater, breathe out, head above water, breathe in, my nose fills with water, it stings. Don't grab the wall, just breathe. Head underwater, one, two, three.

It's still light out when I get home. The kids are lying on the rug with my mother, surrounded by papers and maps. Mom, we found your old drawings! Skulls, cubes, croquis, draperies, sometimes figure drawings, cartoon characters, sketch notebooks, tempera, acrylic, pastel, charcoal. Some of them are quite good. Mom, who's this boy? I take the paper from her hand. It's unlined, the edges are torn, and there's a rip in the middle. The drawing is in blue pencil, Andi's writing is in black. He used to be so hideous and stubby. But now . . . he is fucking fine!!! Not so much his face, but his BODY! It's nice and hard . . . muscular . . . tan . . . and smooth! What are you laughing at, Mom? Nothing. Tell us what you're laughing at! It's just a funny note. Who's this boy? Mom, show me. She wants to tear the paper from my hand. His name is Iván. And why did you draw him? Because I drew all my classmates in eighth grade, and then Andi wrote about them. What did she write? Just that he's good at soccer. That's it? That's the gist of it, I answer. He has blue eyes, I read in my head, but you can't see them nowadays, because he's always sleepy. His clothes are so unbelievably lame. Sometimes he looks like an old person in slippers and cargo shorts. He's either holding his dick with his right hand or rubbing his stomach. Jani started this, and now all the other boys do it. Mom, why are you laughing so hard? I take a picture of the drawing, as well as the note, but in the end I don't send it to Iván. We'll see each other tomorrow, anyway.

Mom, is this Jesus? No, that's Jim Morrison. He was my favorite singer. Did they hang him on a cross too? Why would they hang him on a cross? Because that's how he's holding his arms. They didn't hang him on a cross. And who's that? That's Janis Joplin. She had a nice, rugged voice, but let's have our dinner so I can read you the rest of the story. The prince survives, the older one says. The little mermaid saved the prince, but he didn't know it. That's sad, I say. Mom, was this guy a singer too? I grab the piece of paper, it's a photocopy of a Donatello statue. No, he was a prophet. Then why did you draw a heart on him? Because he looked like the boy I liked. Was he bald too? No, he wasn't bald, but let's go have dinner, okay? Mom, will you draw us? They look at me with big eyes. Their skin is smooth, their noses straight, their eyebrows as delicately curved as Péter's. I look at the shape of their heads, the proportions, who has a higher forehead, or a wider mouth, or a narrower face. In their expressions, I only see Péter. Where am I? Why did I disappear?

I know where you're headed, said the sea witch when she saw the little mermaid. I'm sitting in the middle, the kids on either side, my mother on one end. You want to be free of your tail in exchange for two clumsy legs so the handsome prince will fall in love with you. But it will hurt a lot. Yes, it will feel like swords slicing into your flesh. If you can stay calm and go through all this suffering, then I will be able to help you. I can take it, the little mermaid said in a quavering voice. But I need something in return, said the witch. You have to give me your voice. But if I give you my voice, the little princess stammered, what will I have left? You'll have a nice, slim figure and a bouncing gait, eyes that speak for themselves, said the witch. That's enough to steal a man's heart. The little mermaid took the potion, but she couldn't say anything, because she could no longer speak or sing. Mom, go on! Why are you crying, Mom? Because she's an idiot! Such an idiot. Mom, don't use bad words! She's doing something stupid. She should have never given up her voice. She doesn't know the prince, she just thinks she likes him. Don't cry, Mom. The prince chooses her in the end, I saw it on TV. She still shouldn't have done it. Go on! Go on already! My mother takes the book from my hands. She gets into it, uses a different voice for every character. I gaze out the window, and it still looks like winter, the trees are bare. My mother's right, there won't be any spring this year. I look at my phone, it's Iván. Sorry, I have to cancel tomorrow. Something came up. He doesn't even write what. It's unfortunate that I can't take it lightly.

Andi invited Iván to her eighteenth birthday party. He came by himself, even though he had a girlfriend, not a very pretty one, although as Andi said, she was graceful. I don't remember how Iván ended up kissing me. It's even possible that I kissed him. I'm certain that we had been standing in the kitchen, and that Andi took a photo of us afterward. It was a terrible picture of me, but I didn't throw it out. I still have it, and I no longer see it as terrible, though it's undeniable that I don't look my best. My eyes are red, but I look happy, sprightly, and fresh, or maybe just young, which hides the fact that my face, or rather my expression, is a little off. I'm not wearing a bra, you can see my nipples clearly, but at the time this didn't bother anyone. In fact, it was normal that girls with small breasts like mine didn't wear bras. Iván is standing next to me in a green shirt. He has his arm around me, and he's smiling, his head tilted to one side, like when he used to play the piano. He's looking at me, and I'm looking into the camera. We'd already had a lot to drink, champagne with Red Bull, listening to the Red Hot Chili Peppers and Daft Punk, and by Jani's request, we played "Horny" on the hour. In fact, Jani was sitting at the kitchen table, measuring out weed on a little golden scale. Supposedly Jani only has one testicle, but I could never picture this. The house was full of people, as we were also celebrating Andi's older brother's birthday, it was a joint party, that's how they'd described it to their parents. The next thing I remember, Iván and I were kissing on the rug in Andi's parents' bedroom. Naked. Me underneath. Iván on top. He thinks I was on top. As far as we remember, we had locked the door. I'm certain that Iván wasn't inside me, but I knew that soon he would be. Maybe I was playing with his hair. I remember his soft, silky touch, and Iván remembers stroking my butt, that's why he insists that I was on top. In any case, the door opened, and Andi's brother came in with his friends. Maybe we hadn't locked it properly, or we hadn't locked it at all, it's even possible that Andi's brother got in with a spare key. This is the older brother who fell in love with the girl because she swung on the swings in a sexy way. They came in and saw us, but they didn't turn back. One of them asked if we wanted a little something, another added that cocaine is the best thing for sex. We threw on our clothes and left the room. I looked back through the doorway. The friend who'd offered the coke was leaning over the table. I hoped that, despite this interruption, we might be able to continue, we could go somewhere else, or at the very least, Iván would put his arm around me and we'd laugh, but all I saw in him was distraction. As if nothing had happened. He never said that he felt guilty because of his graceful-though-not-so-pretty girlfriend, though I knew that was what this was all about. The next year, we met at the Sziget Festival. I knew they'd broken up. Andi had told me the story the first day when we ran into Jani and Iván on the train. They talked us into going to the Faithless concert with them. I thought that would be our night. That's when he introduced the sporty girl. Children, I say unto you, that you should eat before any party, do not drink wine from plastic jugs, and do not bring your childhood crushes into your marriage. Listen to my words, listen to your mother.

Vera, this story is terrible. Here's a beautiful girl that the prince dresses up like a boy and then places on a velvet cushion in the window, like she's some kind of dog. He even tells her he longs for another woman, and once he finds her, he has the little mermaid carry her wedding train. Now, children, in this case one should stop everything, because there's just no point. She should find a different man who values her. Poor mermaid, she's completely mute, her legs are bleeding, the prince marries another woman, yet she just keeps smiling. Your mother is right, one should never let themself become mute, remember that! And now the sisters urge her to kill the prince. This Andersen is merciless. Will she die? Who? The mermaid. If she doesn't kill the prince, yes. Is she going to kill the prince? I don't think so, my mother says, and then she goes on reading. The little mermaid threw herself into the sea, and she felt her body slowly dissolve into little clusters of foam. She died? Wait, there's more. Above the sea, she could see little soft, translucent beings gliding past. The little white blotch of foam began to grow, and the mermaid was slowly lifted out of it, and then she could see that she had a body like the rest of them. Where am I, she asked, and her voice hummed so smoothly, like those of the other beings. Her voice came back? It appears so. She didn't become a person, but at least she got her voice back, and her soul became eternal.

The rhythm is the most important. Once you find it, it will work. I focus, I breathe out, and I kick off. My head is deep under the water, that helps with the current. My mother was right, I need better swim goggles. My ear hurts. I should fix my swim cap, but I'm afraid I'll fall out of rhythm. With long strokes, I move forward. One, the tempo of my right hand, I keep exhaling the air in my lungs, two, the tempo of my left, my elbows up high, my arm at my ears, my fingers touching the water first, my heels lined up with each other. I claw gently. I breathe out, but it won't be enough, I can feel where it gets trapped inside, I pull together all my strength, I press on, pulling the water, turning, and by the third time I'm reaching forward again with my right hand. I turn my head to one side, and I can breathe in, because I pushed out all the air from my lungs. Pull, two, three, turn, breathe. The oxygen runs out, I become dizzy, like when I drink cold water too quickly in the summer. The water pours into my mouth, I swallow. My strokes fall apart, I cough, struggle to find the rhythm. My right foot cramps, I try to flex it, it hurts to be kicking in one place. I arrange my movements. My shoulders loose, my arms outstretched, my elbows high. I'm moving forward.

VI. Without any sort of transition comes the heat wave. I'd forgotten how unbearable the house can be in the summer. My father and I closed the blinds, but now there's no airflow. My mother brings over a fan. After canceling our plans for the third time, Iván disappeared. I'll call you right back. He never called. He might be scared that I have expectations, that I want him to leave Judit. But it's not about that. Regardless, I miss him. Particularly the sex. I would like to at least touch myself, but the kids are here, snoring in the room. I even told Andi I miss having sex. Why don't you write Márk, she asks. What Márk? You know, the actor. Márk and Andi went to the same high school. Márk sang in the school band, the Shattered Bricks, and his younger brother Gergő played the guitar. We formed our own little friend group back then. Why him exactly? He just got divorced. If you want to fuck, you're better off with him.

A week later, I'm watching Márk from the third row. I think over what I should write to him. Hi, congratulations. The show was awesome, I really liked your part. It's too bad they kill you in the second act, I would have liked to see more of you. Do you want to go for a drink or something?

Hi, remember me? We danced all night once on the Pest Nights Stage at the Sziget. Andi told me you have a nice dick. Care to fuck?

Hi, I saw your last show. Care to fuck?

In the end, I just write that I saw him in a play, and I congratulate him. He writes back, that's kind of you. I present myself confidently, relaxed. Let's meet up, he writes, we can have a Coke, to which I answer, I don't like Coke, but I'd be up for a glass of wine anytime, to which he says, come over to my place. See, I tell Andi, that's what's good about getting older. There aren't any unnecessary pleasantries. If we both want sex, the road is clear.

How does my butt look? I ask the kids while I stand in front of the mirror. Nice, says the older one. Now, be honest! A little fluffy. What do you mean, fluffy? Just a little fat. Mm-hmm. So not tight? Not really. Maybe a little flat, fluffy's a bit too much. I ask them to take a picture of it, and I try to stand in a way that makes it look best. Péter calls, he'll be here in a half hour to pick up the kids. Instead of going to the zoo, we're going to the pool, so please pack their swim stuff, he says. He picked them up from kindergarten twice last week. They got ice cream and played soccer in the park, and I got to go swimming.

I lie in the tub. I spent a lot of time deliberating which mask I'd put on. One of them has active charcoal to clean the skin all the way to its deepest pores, and it has a gentle, calming effect, whereas the other one contains cucumber extract, has a freshening effect, and makes the skin silky and hydrated. I chose the latter. Once the mask dries, I peel it carefully from my face, starting from my chin and pulling upward. It hurts. If I were to pull it more quickly, it wouldn't hurt as much, but I don't want it to tear. I'm not compulsive. One should eat only after the train departs, the cabinet doors should remain closed, alarms should not be set on the hour. At this age, one can say this of oneself. It's easier to peel the mask from my nose, although since I put less on my forehead, I have to be careful there. It works, and I'm satisfied, like when I blow out the candles all at once on a birthday cake. I squish together the clear film, and it becomes a sticky little clump, like a ball of snot.

Tight butt, shapely legs. I click on the link. Did you know? Eighty-five percent of men consider a nice, tight butt sexy. Eight-five percent. Péter didn't care at all. He never slapped it, never grabbed at it, although he was the only one who truly valued my breasts. Not only did he value them, he even painted them. We'd gotten off the HÉV at Filatorigát, he met my eyes, and we wandered slowly over the rocks. You can take it off, he whispered in my ear. It was huge graffiti, blue and pink circles, it took up two of the walls. Your breasts. Wow, they're big. I stammered, and in my nervousness I forgot I should be glad. After giving birth I looked at my breasts, which were swollen with milk. I showed them to Péter, he should also take a look at them, they'd never been like this before, I needed a bra two sizes bigger. He was sitting in front of the TV, messing with the remote. He glanced up. They are. Come here, grab them! He didn't. I went over so that he would be forced to pay attention to me. He smiled, but he didn't touch them. For years, only the kids reached for my breasts. Once I was done breastfeeding, they were like two withered plums. One day in November, I was washing up in the kitchen. Your age is starting to show, he commented offhandedly. You have wrinkles around your eyes. And am I right that your breasts are drooping? Yes, you are. Of course, it still hurt that he said it. How he said it.

The water starts to cool. I give it a little more hot

water. Is it really possible that I don't remember his dick? I used to mark the days we had sex by putting stars on my calendar. If I'd climaxed, I added an exclamation point. After giving birth, I started to do this less and less. A mother shouldn't act like a whore. I don't know how a whore acts, but regardless, it didn't used to be a problem if I cried out or gave him head. Later, if I embraced him, he'd stroke my arm lightly, but when I pressed my hips against him, he'd say that I was being aggressive.

It was already toward the end, long after the pasta episode. He was watching TV, I was folding clothes. I've realized you're not explicitly aggressive, but your aura is too strong. What do you mean, I asked. You have pheromones radiating off you. You should get a hold of yourself. I can't do anything about that. You're the only one who can do something about it, he answered, and he went back to fiddling with the remote. And what should I do? Supposedly you're an intelligent woman, or at least you claim to be. I'm sure you can come up with something, he said offhandedly. I watch porn, I said. You're disgusting. I felt that he was right. I stood up, and he flinched. I should tell him what I watch, in detail. He should know. He put down the remote. His expression had changed. You just like the lesbian stuff, don't you? You like it when they eat each other out, or when they fuck each other with big plastic dicks. I got up to leave the room, but he called to me, stay, and he squeezed my hand around his hard dick.

I don't want to, I said, and I removed my hand. He pulled it back. His expression wasn't forceful, more so pleading. I think I felt sorry for him. Though I'm not sure I did. But the feeling was similar, maybe a mix of pity and some kind of victoriousness. What exactly had turned him on was unclear. Maybe he had imagined one woman sitting on another woman's face. Or maybe it was knowing that his wife watched porn, that disgust in itself. The way he'd said I was disgusting. Or maybe even the fact that he'd said it aloud. I tugged to a rhythm, up, down. I wanted to do it well, not just get it over with quickly, but make him feel even more ashamed afterward. Because I was sure that he would be ashamed. His face scrunched. On the TV, they were preparing a roasted duck breast with apple marmalade. He climaxed. I tried to wash it off my hands in the bathroom. Sticky clumps formed on my skin. I ran the water for a while, then dried my hands with a towel.

I stop for a bottle of wine on the way, and I spend a lot of time deliberating over it so I don't seem like too much of a snob. Márk lives in Zugló, it takes almost an hour to get there. It hasn't cooled down, even at night, I had to bring a little fan with me. I try to stop myself from becoming nervous, because then I'll sweat and start to smell. My hair is making me even hotter, but I don't pull it back, because the blue dress I'm wearing looks good with my hair down. I text Iván saying that I'm on my way to a date. Péter sends pictures from the pool.

How thoughtful. I used to have to beg for weeks. I start scrolling, but I don't have the patience, so instead I just try to memorize the directions. Once I get off the bus it's an eight-minute walk. The bell number is 11, he's on the third floor. Surely there's an elevator. I'll find my way up, then ring the bell, he'll open the door and then I'll say: hey. And then he'll say that too, just hey, and come in. And I'll go in. That's all there is to it. Two kisses. I'll tell him I brought wine, he should put it in the fridge. To which he'll say, I love white wine. Or he won't say anything. He'll bring me into the kitchen, and I'll take off my sandals. You live here? No, that's stupid, of course that's where he lives. Instead, I'll say, so this is where you live? And then I can talk about the apartment, or how it was easy to find my way here, or something like that.

I can't ring the doorbell, because he's waiting in the doorway. He gives me a frank kiss on the cheek, cigarette smell, come on in, he says with a nice smile. He's taller than I remember. He puts the bottle in the fridge and thanks me for bringing it. Then he shows me around the apartment. There are brown built-in cabinets in the living room with little columns screwed into them, maybe colonial. There was a time when everyone had them, except for us, because my mother found them hideous. In the kid's room is a bed, a Spider-Man comforter, a few toys, the same brown cabinets. I should call my father and tell him not to let the kids watch too much TV.

Thirty minutes, that's the limit I always give them. He never limits them. It's not worth calling.

Márk brings over the glasses and pretzel sticks, moving like he's onstage. We drink wine and talk about the kids and divorce, work, his brother, our mutual friends. He talks more, hardly lets me get a word in. And he opens another bottle. Now I talk more, he's completely silent. I don't know if any sex will come out of this. It's possible that he isn't attracted to me. I shouldn't drink too much, because I'm already at the point where I know I'd throw myself at him. We need water. As Andi always says, hydration is important.

He closes the curtains. I hadn't even noticed that we were sitting next to the table in the light. He steps back, observes, then straightens them so that there's not even a crack. He's very precise, now straightening the thick curtains for the third time. It's fine, I say, to which he answers that he wouldn't like the neighbors to see in. That doesn't bother me, it actually turns me on. I shouldn't have said that, I'm starting to get buzzed. That sounds nice, Márk says, we'll open them up afterward. After what? He reaches into his pocket, takes out a little plastic bag. He dusts it off, breaks the seal open, then spreads white powder onto the table. I need this right now. What is it? A bit of coke. Cocaine? Yes. Márk moves it around with his credit card, arranging it with expertise. He divides the powder into fine lines the same way my mother cuts pasta into strips before she makes dumplings. That one's yours, he says, pointing to the longest line. Thanks, but no. Never? I shake my head. I'll still leave it for you. I don't need any. It doesn't matter that I protest, he sets it off to one side. He takes down a thick black plastic straw that had been on top of the cabinet, it's about eight centimeters long. He puts it to his nose, leans over and snorts the powder. I always hated that gesture. I find it pathetic, that they have to bend their backs. I saw Péter do it once, back at the beginning, and I even told him it was pathetic. I remember using that word. He grabbed me in a hug. I won't do it again, Vera. As far as I know, he kept his word. In any case, I never saw it again. I don't find it pathetic when Márk does it. Or at least, I choose not to care. He wipes his nose. What he couldn't snort he rubs into his gums with his index finger. What does that do, I ask. It relaxes you. It would do you some good too. I'm not relaxed enough? You won't feel pain. I'm not talking physical. It won't make you an addict? You can't get addicted to cocaine. I mean physically, he adds. And psychologically? Don't worry about that. A little euphoria. Sometimes you need it. But I don't want to talk you into anything. You absolutely do. You'd look sexy while you do it. And then what happens, I ask. What do you mean? What happens after you snort it? I talk a lot. You've been talking a lot this whole time. At least when I arrived. Because I was doing this before you got here. You're sure you don't want any? I'm sure.

I don't see it having any particular effect on him, he doesn't laugh anymore, he doesn't gesticulate wildly, he occasionally strokes my leg. I'll be right back. In the meantime, you'll take your clothes off? You take them off me, I answer. I'm alone in the room, staring at the white lines on the brown table. I can hear him peeing, that means he'll be able to hear me. I hate when other people can hear it, but I'll have to go eventually. That's why, in Japan, they have stalls that play music. Andi told me that. She talked about Japan for two hours, with an entire speech about the bathrooms. Then, about how you could go into the store because you need rice, and there'd be men in suits flipping through porn catalogs right next to you. She never saw a woman flip through one.

Márk has a strange kiss, he moves his tongue quickly and his saliva is bitter. It could be because of the cocaine. I'll try it, I say. He nods. The comedown is shit, but I'll be here for you, he answers. What do you mean by shit? Depressing. You'll go from really high to really low. But it doesn't last long, don't worry. Well, how long does it last? A half hour or so. Here's a nice little fat line for you. What do I have to do? You've really never snorted anything before? Look, here's the straw. Which of your nostrils is better? I don't understand the question, and he explains that he's asking which one is better at bringing in air. I must have a strange look still, because he adds that people usually have one nostril that's better for snorting. I give it a try. Maybe this one, I answer. Great, then put the straw right there, push it in a little more, then hold your other one closed. I always breathe in, then snort on three. It's important that I breathe out deep, otherwise I can't snort anything. You sound like my swim instructor, I say. Now he has a strange look, but I don't explain. I think of movies where fallen women snort coke in the bathroom and then rub their noses with their index fingers. I don't remember a straw in their hands. Wait, I say, what if I pass out or something? You're not going to pass out. You don't know that. I've never tried it before, I could be allergic or something. You won't pass out. You'd call an ambulance if I needed it? You're not going to pass out. Promise me you'll take me to the hospital. I promise. Okay, then I'll do it. Wait, wait. If you've never tried coke before, you should try snorting without it so that you figure out the rhythm. One, two, three, after I say three, not when I say three. I move my head with it, that's important. I hold my left nostril closed, and he holds the straw. I almost brush the stuff away with my hair, he sucks in air through his teeth. Careful, that's expensive as fuck! Now, here. Breathe out, straw on the table, one, two, three, breathe in.

Nervous? asks the taxi driver. What do you mean? You keep looking at your watch. I have to get home before the kids wake up. Had a nice party? Does it look that bad? I ask. Don't worry, sometimes you've got to let off steam.

The kids are asleep. I lie down next to them, I'm still shaking a little, I close my eyes. Just a few minutes, I think. They wake me up, we're going to be late, they cry. I don't care. The faster you get ready, the sooner we'll be at school, I say in a calm voice, and meanwhile last night flashes back. He couldn't get it up. What's wrong with this shirt? I cut the tag off. The bear one is in the dirty clothes. The kitty one is also very cute. Go over to the dresser and pick one. I'm not getting one for you, you can go over there. Was it the cocaine? Something about how it wasn't me and that I shouldn't worry. I wasn't worried. Or was I? What's wrong with these pants? Last week they were too big. Then get another pair. Okay, I guess you're going out in your underwear. I'm pretty sure I only had one line. He did the rest of them. Come on, we're going to miss the bus. Okay, then we're walking there. Then you'll have to go without me. After the second bottle of wine, he opened a third. Except it wasn't exactly wine. It was some kind of awful Ukrainian liquor, but I don't think I had any. Yes, I'm picking you up today. Tomorrow Grandpa will. Dad too, yes. Did we even make it to the bed?

I'm ten minutes late for the Monday team meeting that's supposed to start the week. My boss looks at his watch, I'm sorry, I say, and he nods. They're talking about when we should send the newsletter, what should be on the ad, and when the ad should go up on the website. I try to maintain a thoughtful expression. Are you alive? Márk asks. Yes, but I'm a corpse, I answer. Iván messages. Did I really go on a date, or did I just say that to get back at him for canceling our plans twice? Three times, and yes, I answer. I love how you sucked on it, Márk writes. The balcony flashes back, the lights, the blue curtains, the neighbors. Had I wanted to go out there, or was it him?

Andi also checks in. So, how did the night go? Superb, I write. Superb is my grandmother's word, but I've used it since she died. Impignorate, bumfuzzle, bamboozle, brouhaha. I've never had the chance to use brouhaha. Andi is insistent. Details? We drank a lot, we had a lot of sex, and I came. To be continued? I don't know. But would I like it to continue? Dangerous to say, I answer, to which she asks, you've fallen for him already?

I remember kneeling on a chair while he licked me from behind. No one's ever licked me from behind. Ever. Definitely not Péter, he hasn't done any of that in years. A few weeks after the pasta incident, he suggested that the next time we had a free weekend, we should stay home and, as he said it, fuck. It sounded strange to me because Péter doesn't use that word. Make love maybe, rarely sex. I sometimes considered him romantic for that reason, otherwise prudish. Because he said fuck, I thought we could speak openly. I stroked him. Does that mean you'll lick me? Because I'm dying for someone to do that. Something of that nature. He pushed me away from him. Not even a dirty whore would say a thing like that! I was surprised to learn that even Andi thought I'd phrased it crudely. I've since mulled over how I could have phrased it differently, more refined. Would you please kiss my vagina? Could you do it with your tongue down there? Of course, it could be that the words weren't the issue. He'd give me a pinkie when I needed his whole arm. Andi must have come to a similar conclusion, because she asked if I'd wanted to provoke him subconsciously. I answered no, but spent a long time churning over it, and eventually I came to the conclusion that yes, I probably did want to. Iván apologizes for canceling so many times, he didn't want to, believe him, his kid got sick, and Judit finally snapped about how she's always stuck at home and can never go out anywhere. Quite fair, I write, to which he says, of course you'd take my wife's side. I only know Judit from pictures, a Jewish woman with long curly hair. I never found her particularly attractive, but Andi thinks I'm jealous. She's not ugly at all, though her features are a lot sharper. And every part of her is big. Her breasts, her butt, her mouth. Iván often sends me screenshots of their texts. I usually agree with Judit, and because of this Iván feels like we're both secretly conspiring against him.

Judit calls Iván Bear, and he calls Judit Bunny. Sometimes Bunny Ears, or Bun. Bun bothers me most.

A date comes up, and I write it in the calendar so it looks like I'm paying attention. Andi gave me a fan from Japan. Uchiwa. It has a handle and it's stiff. This is what I fan myself with. People in Japan usually use these when they go out because they're more effective at cooling you down and they have nice advertisements. Mine flaunts a five-person boy band. My boss addresses me, I need to ask someone something, I nod. Márk writes: rather dirty things happened last night, that's how he writes it, dirty, in English, but I don't know what he's referring to. I ask, he doesn't answer. Or rather, he doesn't answer the question. Maybe I said something vulgar that turned him on, or he said something vulgar that turned me on. Iván doesn't give up: we can plan to meet tomorrow. Márk says goodbye because he has to buy a Jedi action figure for his son. An image flashes back. I'm kneeling on the floor, pretending I'm a prostitute who gives head for cocaine. I sweat. I go to the bathroom and wash my face and hair thoroughly, splash water on my neck, hold my wrists under the faucet, then take a few sips. The image of last night becomes clearer in places. A feeling of shame crawls up my stomach.

At four o'clock I go to the kindergarten. I fall asleep on the bus, and a man steps on my foot, that's why I get off in time. Elvira néni calls me over to talk privately.

The little one wet her pants, this is now the third time, we should keep an eye on it. I nod. The psychologist said that for the first six months every reaction can be considered normal, I say. Or maybe I just think it to myself. She pats my arm, she knows it's hard. I should try valerian, I can get it without a prescription. It's important that I sleep.

There's a large bouquet of roses at the front door. Maybe for the neighbor, delivered to the wrong place. Or someone sent them to my mother. My mother hasn't lived here for years. I could also get flowers. My father, unlikely. Some coworker? The bouquet is over the top. It must be Iván. He senses that this date thing isn't going anywhere good, and now he has to win me back. Mom, look, it's Cinderella! I hold it in my hand, it looks like a Kinder egg figurine. I got Snow White, the little one shouts, and she kisses it. Dad brought them, she says. For our anniversary. I hadn't even remembered.

I don't want any coke, I tell Márk. I'm fanning myself with the uchiwa fan, it's the only breeze. His toenails are long. It bothers me. I would love to tell him to cut them, but right now we don't have that kind of relationship. He texted me that morning, how about I come over to his place? Iván is convinced I canceled on him out of spite, but if Márk hadn't called, I would have absolutely met up with him. It's strange that I didn't waver more. In fact, I didn't waver at all. What do I think of his body, he asks. It's not bad, I answer. He's offended that I'm not more enthusiastic. He got a minor part in a Chinese action film, he's lifting all the time. He really does have a nice body, better than any other guy I've been with. Péter is thin, but he gained a few kilos after our wedding, which all went to his stomach. Iván's 120 kilos. Or 130, I don't know. He's big. I don't want to drink a lot, I tell Márk while he pours me a glass of wine. But you need it with the coke, otherwise you'll get too wound up. Nothing bad happened before, I think to myself while he places my heel against his dick. I can just have one line.

# VII.

Good. But not just good. Unbelievably good. Stunningly and dizzyingly and mind-blowingly and inexplicably good, I would explain to Andi if she asked what doing cocaine felt like. There's no pain, no tiredness, no sadness. Your words just suddenly fall into place in a way that makes sense, you don't have to search for them, everything is simple and easy. That's about what I would say. Also that space is key. That and time. Space expands, time disappears. I would say this too, and while I don't like big words, Andi would not let me leave it at that, because what does space expanding look like, and she'd ask: what do I mean by time disappearing? I shouldn't just list the generic, I need concrete examples. It's concerning the body, I would stammer. There's no mass, no outlines, no borders. The sky and all its stars are in my chest. So there are outlines? So you do feel your body? Or how else would you know there are stars in your chest? I would be irritated with all her questions, that she isn't satisfied with the star metaphor, but I'd try to explain it again some other way. What I'm certain of, I'd start, is that every motion is directed upward. So you're flying, she'd ask, and then I'd answer, I'm not flying, I'm just up there. She would give an mm-hmm, and I'd continue with the concept of time. How do you know it disappears, she'd ask, and I'd wonder how I know it even exists. If I was shut in a room without windows all by myself, how would I know that time was passing? I'd talk. And if I were mute? I'd pace around the room. And if I couldn't move? I'd count my heartbeats. That's how I know time disappears, I'd say to Andi, because I can't hear my heart beating. Not only do I not hear it, I don't even feel it. There's nothing that would indicate the passing of time. Or maybe she wouldn't ask that at all, maybe she'd just want to know why.

Andi thinks everything's going great with Márk. And really a lot of things are good. We know when the other person wakes up, how they slept, what they dreamed about, and how put out they're feeling that day. We exchange pictures of our thermostats, because we're competing over whose place is hotter. He calls me little chick, sexy little chick, sometimes Pretty One, Hey, Pretty One, just like that. Or maybe My Pretty One. He says I have excellent legs. He's interested in my work, and pretty soon he can tell my coworkers apart. That's the one who's always sniffling, now that's the one who talks too much? Sometimes he writes that he misses me. Whenever he does, he'll either look at pictures of me or go back and reread our texts. Andi thinks that's cute. I think so too. He's honest. Or at least he can be honest. He told me he sees other women. Sometimes I'm afraid that I'm falling in love with him. Sometimes I'm afraid that he won't fall in love with me.

Péter called asking me what I think about him taking the kids on a trip for a week. There'd be a lot of people coming, and then he listed a few of our mutual friends, who are no longer our mutual friends, just Péter's friends, then he adds, everyone's bringing their kids. I was quiet, because I didn't want to be too quick to say of course, take them, so that he wouldn't think I'm the kind of mother who would just send off her kids, and he seemed to think he had to convince me, bringing up all sorts of reasons, I'm sure they'll have a lot of fun, it'll be a sandy beach, and I shouldn't worry, it's mostly shallow, it doesn't drop off, and of course they'd be happy, notice the plural case, if I come too. All I answered was, of course, Péter. You can take the kids. Go ahead and take them, for two weeks if you want, or even a month, although this I just thought to myself. I already suggested to my mother that they spend two weeks at Lake Balaton instead of the usual one. There's nothing stopping you, she answered. And I felt that sometimes life can be that simple.

Nowadays one bag isn't enough. Márk makes the call around midnight, climbs into the taxi, and gets some more from the dealer. He calls them from my phone because he hasn't paid his phone bill. The dealer's number is hidden in my contacts under the name Tonic. I've never spoken to Tonic, Márk takes care of all the communications and the funds. I don't hand out money for drugs.

Márk comes down faster than I do. He becomes quiet, lies down and pulls a comforter over himself, even in the worst of the heat. Tell me a story! About what? Whatever, I just don't want it to be quiet. I try to memorize his outlines, his proportions, the size of his nose and where his eyebrows end, so that I can draw him at home. If he's really having a hard time, I'll kiss his neck, bite at his nipples, that sort of thing. Sometimes he'll say that he's never had that good of a comedown. It feels good to hear that, even if it's not true. It hits me differently. I can't breathe through my nose. I don't have any saliva, no matter how much water I drink, my mouth is still dry. I'm not capable of forming words with my tongue, the muscles in my face stiffen. I'm constantly blowing my nose, and then it starts to get chapped, burns, and stings. Next time I'll bring nose spray, I always tell Márk, but once I get to the pharmacy, I think of Andi. She was addicted to nose spray for years. Nasivin, Novorin, Otrivin, Rhinospray. Better to have a bit of discomfort during the comedown than have an addiction to nose spray.

Part of that discomfort includes the shakes and chattering teeth. My heart starts pounding, and I'm convinced that I'm dying. I even tell Márk to take me to the hospital, to which he says, chill, it'll pass soon. He's right, it always passes. If he senses that I'm doing better, he gives me a kiss, turns onto his other side, and falls asleep. It doesn't matter that he's sleeping next to me, I still feel alone. The shaking doesn't stop the next day either. If Andi asked me what it felt like, I'd tell her that it's similar to a panic attack, but that's more like something huge closing in on you, and this is just free fall. From up very high, straight down into a horrible abyss, I'd say dramatically. Into hell, she'd ask, and I would answer that it depends on your version of hell, because if you're thinking of the red-and-black kind, with a little bit of purple, and naked twisted-up bodies screaming in pain among flames, then no, but if you mean a place where there's no solid ground, just cold mud, then you're close. No matter how I tried to put words to it, it became static, and even the colors were bland. It can't all be black. The free fall suddenly stops. The space starts to shrink, it strangles you. Everything is stiff.

At first it only lasted for a day, but now it's usually two, sometimes even three. It's called cocaine depression. Márk says it's caffeine depression, and I call it choco-sadness, because I usually crave chocolate most. I don't swim, I'm never in the mood to talk. I don't have an appetite either. At lunch, I tell my coworkers I had a big breakfast, and then I lie to my father that I ate at work. The kids, the few days that we're together, I put in front of the TV. Then I lie in bed and feel guilty. Can we watch another one, they ask, and I nod, of course, go ahead. I don't answer Iván's messages, and if Andi calls, I don't answer, I just text her that I'm with Márk, or I'm in a meeting, or I'm playing with the kids. Vera, this isn't good, she would say, and I would answer that she shouldn't worry, because I can quit whenever I want.

We couldn't just fuck? I say to Márk. What do you mean? Clean. Without any of that stuff. That's what I say, but really I'm longing to do a line while he fucks me from behind. Márk, I don't want to depend on it. I shouldn't worry, he says, I'm not going to become an addict if I do it three or four times a week. But you're an addict, I say, to which he says, I don't want to talk about that, to which I answer, we are talking about it. Listen, I start calmly. I don't know how many other women you see besides me, and I don't even want to know, but you've done enough coke with me alone to buy us a two-week vacation at the beach. I hope he'll interrupt with Vera, you're the only one for me, but instead he tells me to drop it, to which I answer that I'm not dropping it, and I come back with things like, your mucous membranes will go to shit, because I read on Wikipedia that it'll ruin your blood pressure, and the way it changes your relationship to sex is terrifying, that's the word I use, terrifying, because you'll never want to do it again sober, and the whole thing is unbelievably depressing, because even if you escape, that becomes the prison, and I want to be free, I finish solemnly. You don't have to do any. I, however, need to get high, he answers.

I tell a story from work in detail, as if it were something important. Are you coming, he asks. I look at his feet. Trim your toenails! Oh, come on, just get over here and have some. That nice, fat line is all yours, he says. The straw is in my hand. I start to get wet. I don't want any, I answer. Come on, be a good little girl! It's not like the first time, I say. If we gave it a little time, would it be? We'd have to give it a lot of time, and we don't want that. I want that, I answer, whereas he wants me to drop the act and put the straw to my nose, because he would like to get off already, and this is the best way for him to do it. He hugs me from behind and reaches into my panties, stroking my clit, digging in his finger. I move slowly, and when I really start to feel it, he presses the straw into my hand. I want to see you do it. Do it!

I've wasted the whole summer, la-la-la-la-laaa, I say. I'm drunk, I'm high, it's hot, I'm shaking. You know you're taking me to the hospital if I need it. You're strung out. Just drink a little wine and you'll calm down, Márk says. Not like this, no, no, no. I slap him. I hate that I can't come, I despise being underneath him all the time, look at my back, you've fucked me so hard that it's bruised, and the kids are asking, Mom, what happened to your back, and I tell them that I have no idea, and then they ask, Mom, what happened to your knees, and should I say, well, children, your mother spent the whole night on her knees sucking someone's dick. Vera, finish your fit and have a drink. I didn't call the kids, though I promised to.

Keep going! I want to hear you, Márk says while he fucks me from behind. My mouth is dry, and I look at the table, it's empty, we snorted everything, he rubbed the last few grains into my gums. What do you want to hear? How much I want to snort another line? I want to hear you moan. His dick gets even harder as he says it. And one more, and whatever you put on the table, it'll be gone. Give me more, I yell. He jumps up and reaches for his phone. What are you doing? I'm calling someone. You idiot, it's one in the morning! He might pick up. Don't do this, it was just a joke. You know that's not true, he says, drumming his fingers anxiously. I don't want to stay here by myself, I say, but he's already talking to Tonic. It'll be ten minutes, I'll call a taxi. Just touch yourself until then. I don't need any more, seriously. You might not, but I definitely do, he answers, and he puts on his pants. I'm completely out of cash, can you give me your card? I don't want to, but in the end, I give it to him. I'm going out, I'm coming right back, don't fall asleep on me. As if I could sleep in this situation. I turn left, I turn right, I sit up. Nothing works. I should drink a little wine. I look at the empty bottles in the corner, try to figure out which labels I recognize. Which one did I bring, which one is from another woman? I shouldn't think these thoughts. At least he doesn't lie about it. The kid's room is the coolest, that's where we usually sleep. Márk laid a down comforter on the floor, that way the heat is a little more bearable. I hate this apartment. It's always the same. Elevator, wine in the fridge, table, chair, closed curtains, straw, glasses. Last time I suggested we go out to see a movie. Or go out for dinner, walk around the neighborhood. We will, he answered, but we never go anywhere. I pull back the curtains. Márk comes home and closes them. What, did you give the neighbors a show? Do you want to meet my kids, I ask, but I don't wait for the answer. We could go for a hike, we could play with Legos. I see you've opened another bottle. I hate these curtains. What if we left them open? Are you okay? he replies. He undresses and sits at the table. I stare at the ceiling, listen to his movements, try to judge where he is. He sniffs, wipes his nose, pulls his chair closer, waves the bag, flicks it, smiles at me. He should be opening the bag, but I don't hear him do it. Why isn't he opening it? Catch! He tosses the baggie at me. Come on, have some. That's Márk's job, just like the dealer and the money. I sit at the table and move around the powder. I stroke it, press it, draw it into different shapes. Márk gets impatient. That's enough. I snort two lines, one after the other.

What was that? What? What you did with my neck. I thought you liked it. It hurt. I know. You knew it hurt, so you kept doing it? You were getting into it. Why do you say that? The noise you made, and you got so wet. No, I didn't. Yes, you did. You need to let go, he says, and he starts to stroke my neck, then squeezes it lightly. I want to push away his hand, but instead I just lean into it. It's strange, but there's something exciting in it. That it hurts. Or that he knows it hurts and does it anyway. It's like coke, him squeezing my neck tighter and tighter. Stop, I say. He lets go. That's scary. What I did, or that you liked it? It's sick. I don't want to get off on something that hurts. Vera, it's just sex. But why should I like that it hurts? And why do you like that it hurts me? As soon as you tell me it hurts, I'll stop. If I say it does, it'll turn you on. Because it turns you on, he answers.

Just try to breathe! Now, stay calm, take a deep breath, then breathe out, Vera, breathe out! I'm not taking you to the hospital, you'll be fine in a second. I'm not pulling back the curtains. But you are breathing, just open your mouth! Look at me. Everything is going to be fine. Come on, drink some water. It's fine, just drink. You're not going to throw up. You were just freezing. I'm here, I won't let anything happen to you. You aren't going to die. Blow your nose, it'll stop bleeding. You just broke a vein, that's all. It'll pass, believe me. It'll be over soon. Breathe.

## VIII.

Buzzer, elevator, I fix my hair in the mirror, dab the sweat from my neck and cheeks, everything is normal, except that Márk isn't waiting for me. I ring the bell, nothing. Just as I think to ring again, he opens the door. Black sweatpants, a white long-sleeved shirt. What, are you cold? I ask. I hug him, I open the wine, pull back the curtains, he doesn't protest. I start to fan myself with the Japanese boy band. Márk seems tired, his gestures are dull. He has a hostile look, or maybe I'm just imagining it. I try to be smooth and relaxed, I talk a lot. He sits with his legs crossed, his back hunched. He smokes one cigarette after another and doesn't look at me. Alternates between wringing his hands and biting his fingernails.

What's your problem anyway, I ask after a while. We don't have to talk. If you want, we can sleep. That's not what I meant. Then what did you mean? Never mind, forget it. He avoids my gaze. Is it that we don't have any cocaine? I don't say coke, or stuff, or party favors, I specifically say cocaine, and I can see that he's surprised. It sounds strange to me too, a lot worse than if I'd asked: is it that we don't have any coke? I came over because I wanted to be with you. We don't have to have sex, I say. It was a bad idea to come. Márk had explicitly told me not to, and I threw a fit.

It started in the morning with me taking a look around the room. I'd come home as the sun was rising, my father had been looking after the kids. There were crumpled papers and the remains of soggy choco puffs on the brown side table. And, on the floor, crumbled cookie bits, pebbles, pencils, a ton of Legos, and a large pile of dirty clothes stacked right in the middle of the room. I removed two caked bits of cocaine from my nose while brushing my teeth, then stood on the scale, forty-five kilograms, I thought about how I should eat. I gazed into the mirror, plucked out a few gray hairs, thought about how I am aging. I woke up the kids, they need to clean this up now, I'm tired of always picking up after them, I said without any sort of lead-up and in an angry tone, the room is full of junk, I can't keep it organized like this, I'm going to pick out five stuffed animals right now, and we're going to take them to kids in need, and after that, not a single stuffed animal will set foot in this house, because I'll toss them all out the window. It would have been easier if they had cried. The little one shouted, uh-oh, here comes the Wrath of Mom, while the older one announced, great, so then we can still have fish plushies, because they don't have feet. I should have laughed, or at least, it would have been better if I could have laughed. I played up the Wrath of Mom, I used my gruff voice, enough stalling, we're cleaning up, now. Instead came the clenched fists, the image of me dragging them by their hair, smacking them in the face, shoving them to the floor, stomping on them, digging my nails deep into their skin. Father Lajos's voice, go to the bathroom, pray to the Holy Spirit, Andi's voice, what are you doing? Péter's voice, you can see, Your Honor, that she is not fit for the role of mother, Márk's voice, Vera, it's all okay, just calm down, my voice, stop this, stop this. I didn't stop. I yelled, I grabbed the little one, she tried to tear herself from my grasp. I squeezed her harder, did you not hear what I just said, stop it, let me go, she yelled, I squeezed her even tighter, she struggled, she hit me, she kicked at my thighs, do not kick me, you understand, we don't hit anyone, we never hit anyone, I shook her, I threw her down onto the bed. The older one shouted, Mom, stop it! I stormed to the Legos, I belted, pick this up now, every last piece. I didn't put them there, she said, to which I answered, I don't care who put them there, pick them up and put them in the box, otherwise I'm throwing everything into the trash, to which she said, you wouldn't throw them out. And that's when I grabbed what had taken days for all of us to put together, the house, the three beds, the tub, the toilet, the wardrobe, the backyard pool, the observatory, the connecting bridge, the piano and the carousel, the palm tree, the pine tree, I grabbed it all, I lifted it up, and I threw it to the ground with all my strength. All three of us started to cry. That's how it started, and that's how it ended with me telling Márk that we had to meet up. He said I could come over, but the night would have to be on me, because he was fresh out of cash. We can't do it without the party favors? I asked. We can't just talk and go to sleep, to which he said, that's the joke of the year, to which I answered, I'm sick of not being able to hang out with him sober, to which he then said, it's not that simple, because he's been drying up in the apartment all day at 35°C and sure, it'd be nice for us to sleep together, but wouldn't it be better if we fucked? And that we absolutely cannot do without the party favors. I would be fine with just sleeping, I wrote, to which I added, but I'm not going to force it, even though I knew that was what I was doing. I'll think about it, give me ten minutes. Ten minutes is a long time, I answered, as if I were so cool and confident, while really I knew the whole thing was pathetic. Nine minutes later, he said, come over, and bring some wine. And I left home as cheerfully as I had in high school whenever my father let me go to a house party.

Márk starts to soften up. He smiles, he even laughs, his legs are no longer crossed. The wine helps. I kiss him, he lets me. I head for the shower, he pulls me back. It's good that you're here. He seems genuine. I stroke his face. I was scared, he continues. About what it would be like to hang out like this. I was afraid we'd mess it up, that you'd mess it up. That I'd mess it up? What are you talking about? That it wouldn't be as good without the party favors, he answers. That it would be different, boring. You were afraid that having sex with me wouldn't be good unless we were on something? You don't get it, he says, his expression profoundly sad. Are you afraid that you'd be boring? He doesn't answer. Chill, we don't have to have sex. Don't tell me to chill, that's not going to help.

After showering I put on panties and Márk's tattered shirt so that he doesn't think I'm expecting anything. I hug him, he kisses me, I play with his hair. He tries to take the shirt off me but my hand gets stuck in it, I sit up, we get it off, he kisses me again. He runs his hand across my stomach, my back, my thighs. It's good so far. Of course, it'd be better if we were on something. Or not better, just different. Finally, his saliva isn't bitter. I feel his touch much more acutely, the beginning and end of his every move, they don't blur together. I take off his briefs, me below, him above, everything is simple. He goes inside me and it feels good, his dick is a lot larger and harder than it usually is, but I don't tell him this. None of that sort of thing, no I want you to fuck me, not even that feels good, or don't stop. We don't say anything at all. Silent, quick, sober sex. I can't leave. If he asked me to give him head on the balcony, would I do it? And if he said I'd get a line if I gave him head on the balcony? That turns me on, I get so wet that he has to wipe himself off on his shirt. He goes back in. I imagine I'm doing a line, and I come.

How was it, I ask afterward. I know I shouldn't ask, but I still do. Not bad, he answers. Not bad? Not bad. But was it good? It wasn't bad, and given the situation, you should take that as a compliment. I've heard better compliments. He turns toward me, props himself up on his elbow. Vera, listen, I was tired and wanted to sleep. I wanted to be alone, but you begged to come over. I didn't beg, I interrupt, though he's right, I did beg, but he doesn't react, he just continues. We talked, we had some wine, we laughed, and I had a good time, I let go completely. If you'd asked me before, I could have never imagined it'd be that way, so there you go. And yes, it wasn't bad, given that I haven't had sex with anyone sober in two years. But if this is what you want to hear, then fine: it was good. We're lying on our backs. I stare at the ceiling with my arms crossed. So it was good, but not as good as when you were high, that's what you're trying to say? He doesn't answer for a while. It was different. I sigh, and we go back to being silent. I turn to him. I enjoyed it. It finally felt real. And it'll be even better. He says nothing. Maybe he thinks I'm lying. He falls asleep quickly, and I can't, though for once I'm not shaking. I don't have to blow my nose, I don't feel nauseated.

A week before we moved in with my father and before I left Péter, I went out partying. One of the guys walked me home, and I was glad I wasn't alone. We chatted for a bit in front of the building. I was drunk, but the happy, soft sort of drunk. I went upstairs and lay in bed next to Péter. You're late, he said. You said you'd be home by midnight. I didn't feel like pointing out that we'd agreed I'd leave by midnight, nor did I want to bring up that over the last few years he had rarely arrived on time anywhere. I said, sorry, and I pulled myself to the edge of the bed and closed my eyes. The room was spinning.

I was lying on my stomach, already half-asleep, when I woke to him hitting me in the head. Later, Péter said he didn't hit me, he just gave me a light tap, like this, a tiny little tap, and he says in a babying voice, I'll give you a knock on the head, but be careful, or you'll get a nice smack, he finishes, and he gives me another tap. It was just a warning. A gentle warning. It wasn't gentle, it was sinister. Or refined, like a slice serve in Ping-Pong. Are you crazy? Maybe that's what I'd asked. He came back at me saying that I came home late, and I was carousing with some other guy in the doorway, the smell of alcohol is radiating off me, and then I have the nerve to lie next to him and sleep. Our relationship is in ruins, this was how he phrased it, ruins, and I just go to sleep. I'm tired, we can talk about this tomorrow. You're not tired, you're drunk. Go to the kids' room, I don't want to be in the same bed as you. You go, and leave me alone, I would like to sleep. I turned away from him. Get the fuck out of here, you bitch, he said, and he kicked me. Are you insane, I asked. He slid down lower and kicked my thigh with his other leg. I sat up, saying, you're sick. You shut your mouth! You've lost your mind. Didn't I tell you to shut the fuck up? He pushed me from the bed, knelt over me, grabbed my hair in his fist, and beat my head against the mattress over and over, hard, until I cried. And then he said, finally, you're crying. And he let me go.

Márk is breathing steadily beside me. I also only calmed down this morning once the kids started to cry. I've never felt that kind of rage toward anyone. Do other mothers ever feel like this? Did my mother ever feel this? When I was a kid, if someone yelled, we pretended like nothing happened afterward. My parents never asked forgiveness if they yelled at me, my grandparents never asked forgiveness if they yelled at my parents. Sometimes my father even got a little tap. That's what they called it, a little tap. A kind word, harmless, like a little clap. There was no sense of pain in it. Péter never apologized to me either. And I never apologized to the kids. We tried to rebuild the house, then we went out for ice cream. We were silent all day. I start crying. I try to be quiet so I won't wake up Márk, and then I try to be loud so that I do. He doesn't wake up. I need to apologize to them.

IX. Do you think she actually appeared? Who? The Virgin Mary. Andi shrugs. Do you? Now I shrug. Look at this big one! She grimaces. How can it be so ugly? I move closer to it. She has such a pathetic inflatable doll head, poor thing. Are you sure you want to buy it? I nod. And a rosary too. For what? So I can give it to my grandchildren with shaking hands and say, this is from Fátima, it will ward off any trouble. That's how I got one from my grandmother, these things are important. Andi looks at the key chains, and I look at the holy water flasks. Look, Jesus is nowhere to be found. Mary really runs this place. Of course, that's understandable, it was a lone mission. Andi mm-hmms. The whole day has been strange. Meaning that I'm the one being strange. She keeps asking me how I'm doing, and I keep saying all good, thanks. Isn't it a little odd that the last big appearance was a hundred years ago, and since then nothing? I continue while picking out a holographic refrigerator magnet that has the three peasant children on it, Lucia, Jacinta, and Francisco, who are on their knees praying to the Virgin Mary floating above a rainbow. Anyways, I'm sure she wasn't this sort of blond, white, weary-eyed princess. I imagine a curly-haired woman with dark skin and a strong figure. So why did she come down to the people in that form? Andi nods to show she's listening. Because she had to fulfill their expectations. Otherwise, they wouldn't have realized who she was. Either way, it's suspicious. Because then she chooses to announce her next appearance. Bold. A real performance, professional, full of bravado. Look at this! Andi hands me a green plastic Virgin Mary figurine with gold-trimmed clothing. The woman running the stand points to the sky and I give a big nod, I'm sure it's been blessed. She wants to show us something, Andi says. Give it to her. The woman takes it, and a moment later the Virgin Mary's body is glowing with green light, like she's some kind of swamp monster.

The space is huge, like a landing strip. A few people bow to their knees, a group of young women are singing spiritual songs. Andi shows me where we can buy candles. We can pick from five different sizes, the largest a half-meter tall, the smallest twenty centimeters. The prices vary depending on the size, the money we throw into a huge offering box. There's nobody watching how much money we put in, we could leave without paying. We don't, one doesn't risk that sort of thing, it is about the souls of our deceased relatives, after all. I count them. My grandparents, four, their siblings, four, my great-uncle on my father's side, my great-aunt's husband on my mother's side, a friend from my kindergarten class, two classmates from elementary school, four former colleagues, three of Péter's friends, my godfather, my mother's best friend, my father's childhood friend and his family, my mother-in-law and my father-in-law. Four suicides, three car accidents, three from alcoholism, one from a pulmonary embolism, the rest cancer.

Everywhere people are holding candles. We duck under the cordon, and nobody speaks, we think of our dead, or other things, like, for example, I think about how this candle thing must be great business for the church, the wax is reusable, and if I remember correctly, Andi said they don't even pay taxes on it. The tall chimney is pouring out smoke, so that Fátima is lingering in the smell of burned tallow. It's hot, and the closer we get to the black structure, the hotter it gets. I light the wicks, set the candles into the iron holders, and I watch how they melt and hunch over in purgatory's heat.

What are these, I ask Andi. There are gray plastic boxes in front of me, similar to the ones we put our bags and suitcases in at airport security, except there are wax body parts in these. Legs, arms, and in one of them, an embryo. A heart, stomach, lungs, a kidney, a woman's breast. Offerings, Andi answers. They buy them, burn them, and hope that they recover. Or they've recovered, and now they're burning them out of thanks. Strange, I say, and I grab one of the tits. Shapely tits, not too big, but bigger than mine. Andi snaps at me to put it back because someone already bought them. Do you think they have a brain too?

I'm not an addict. That's what I kept repeating to myself on the way to Lisbon. Otherwise I wouldn't be here. It was Andi's idea, she arranged it with my mother. I didn't know anything about it. Andi knows me, she knew I'd start looking for excuses, as I have thus far. I don't have money, I can't take off work, and of course, the last resort: the kids. One time Andi even mentioned that it would be more decent of me to not make them into an excuse.

When I was given the plane tickets, I cried. More out of desperation than being moved by them. I'd planned to write everything down. Monday, zoo, rain jacket, sandwich, water bottle, Tuesday, conditioning, leggings, tank top, Wednesday, Fruit Day, I need to get grapes, Thursday, swimming, hair dryer, the older one's grade school prep. I'd wanted to prepare their clothes for each day, but in the end I didn't do anything, just thought about what would happen if I didn't go. If I was to come up with some false obligation to cancel over, or arrange events so that the trip would have to be canceled.

Andi, what do you know about the creation of the world? We're sitting cross-legged on a plaid comforter, the ocean in front of us. Not much, she answers. She opens the second bottle of wine, and I hold out my cup. I would like for someone to tell me the story. Once upon a time, *x* million years ago, this happened, then that. Like I could tell you about what happened yesterday. It would have a beginning and an ending, it would have structure, causes, effects. Aren't you ever scared, I ask Andi. Of what? All of it. That nothing makes sense the way it is. You mean life? I don't answer. Like climate change, that we'll all die, that sort of thing? I nod. I'm not usually. And you're not afraid of the world ending in our lifetime? Nope. The planet will live on for a while anyways, at most mankind will die out. But what if the world ends? Then it ends, she answers. I think God's already sick of it, I say, and I pour myself more wine, because Andi only poured a little. Or I drank it quickly. Obviously, human creativity is exciting to a certain extent, buildings, discoveries, inventions, art, but the stories never change. Someone is always in love, someone is always suffering, and sometimes there are happy moments. Do you think he knew this would happen? I ask. God? I think all he knew was that it would all end eventually, she answers. Andi stretches out her legs and forms a hill from the sand in front of her. Whenever I'm really down, I continue, I remind myself that our existence is important, because the next creation will turn out better. He can test out what works well and then fix the errors. I'm not saying the first one is a complete failure. He came up with a lot of great stuff. It's clear that he had a sense of beauty and that he understands proportions. But a lot of idiotic stuff made it into the system. First Adam, then Eve, because Adam was bored. Bullshit. God was bored. You know what it was? There was no sex, no arguments, no worthwhile thought. An existence without desire. He already suspects that creation didn't turn out as well as it could have, but he doesn't admit it, instead he rather slyly has a snake do the dirty work for him. You may surely eat of every tree of the garden, but of the tree of the knowledge of good and evil you shall not eat. Please, did he not have any pedagogical sense? Was it because of free will? Absolutely not. He knew very well what would happen, but he was going to enjoy himself a little. It would have been more decent of him to just drop the whole charade. But what should we expect? This was the first creation. And while the first is always memorable, it's rarely ever the best.

The air starts to get cold, and Andi takes out a thick blanket. We wrap ourselves up in it. I create a depression in the sand with my butt and rest my back against the mound of sand. It's a lot more comfortable this way. She slices a bit of cheese and hands it to me. I could imagine, I say later, that it's just a game. We have to crack the code so we can move forward. Here's fire, you can move on to the next level, you invented the wheel, move on, paper, loom, jump ahead one space, gas, electricity, internet. And the key is at the end. If we can find it, we escape. But who knows if we're on the right track, maybe these aren't the codes we need to crack. Maybe we need some other sort of knowledge or abilities to escape, and the whole thing is a dead end. It's possible that there are more realities existing simultaneously, and God has us compete against each other. At least, that's what I would do. Andi is silent. I'm sure she's wondering how I pulled all these idiotic ideas together.

Do you remember the first time you saw the sea, I ask Andi. Just that it was salty. I was really small then, but apparently I screamed when they brought me into the water. I remember. We went to Bulgaria as a family. My mom talked about the sea the whole drive, how it was a miracle. Meanwhile the Beatles and Tamás Cseh were playing on the radio. *Antoine and Désiré.* We listened to a ton of stuff, but I never paid attention to the lyrics. There's a song about being blown away by the wind. I remember it clearly. I was sitting in the back seat of the Zsiguli, my father was driving, my mother was unwrapping the sandwiches, and in that moment, I understood the lyrics. *But here's the song, it comes from my mouth, the breeze is a handy cornerstone.* I felt a sort of pepped-up happiness, because something that had been hazy thus far finally became clear. My father shouted, children, we've arrived. There was no other child, he just always referred to me and my mother that way. We had stopped along an elevated winding road with the enormous sea below us. Wow, I said, that's huge. But that's it, I wasn't impressed. I also thought the Balaton was huge. I wanted to get back into the car. I only felt the sea's difference from the Balaton when I went in for the first time. It was frighteningly large and powerful. We were playing Schnapsen in front of the tent that night when my mother said that she would give anything to hear the waves crashing for the rest of her life. She's right, I thought. I've been racking my mind lately about how I'd paint a picture of it. And how would you? Obviously I'd paint the horizon, but the sea is also very vertical. You know how deep it is on average? I don't wait for her to answer, I just toss it out: thirty-seven hundred meters. And the land's average height? No idea, she says. Guess! Fifteen hundred. Eight hundred forty meters. You wouldn't have thought that, would you? Everything on land could fit into the sea's depths.

Andi crumples up her towel and places it under her head, then lies down on the blanket. I wonder if I'll remember this moment later. Or will I forget it, like so many other things I thought I'd remember forever? It's strange, there are so many moments that aren't at all important in themselves, but they still become unforgettable, I say aloud. Like in school, when they announced the republic. We were in English class. I wasn't happy about it because I liked Russian. I liked that word, devushka. Instead, they'd written on the board that Michael Jackson is a singer. The *is* was circled. That's the sentence I was reading when the intercom sounded. And that's how a trivial thing became memorable. I remember when József Antall died, Andi says. Everyone remembers that. We were all watching *DuckTales*, and suddenly the screen went black, and they made the death announcement. Except my cousin thought it was Scrooge McDuck who had died.

I pat down my backrest made of sand and lie on the blanket. My towel is still wet, so I rest my head on my sweatshirt. We're silent. I never want to be anywhere else. I know that feeling will go away soon, but in this moment, it's best to be here. Is it possible to live without seeing the ocean? If I were in Portugal, I'm sure I would think no. I would look at landlocked people with pity. To which I say, what is the ocean to me? Can a person live without seeing Budapest's Three Border Mountain? Isn't it strange, I say aloud, that death is so close? And so vast? What do you mean, Andi asks. I mean the ocean. It can be so alluring. Come on, you'll see I'm calm and comfortable, look, every part of me is smooth, to which I then think, why don't

I go for a little swim? And you go in deeper, because it keeps whispering, yes, isn't my touch so soft, yes, aren't I so beautiful, it's best here, but now it won't let you go easily. You have to know how to say no, otherwise you don't have much of a chance, Andi answers.

Do you think there's ever a time when there aren't any waves, I ask. There isn't. So it's always been like this? Always. It's strange that I've never really heard it before. That's how it is with sounds, she answers, as if she were saying the sun sets every day. The kids come to mind, that sometimes no matter how much they screech, I don't hear them, and yet other times the smallest little argument makes my head explode. You know what's interesting, I say. I was sitting on the metro. I ride it every day, but once it was so loud when it braked that I had to cover my ears. It was a loud screeching, or maybe even shrieking. Maybe chirping. What do you mean? Like, seeeeep, but at a frequency that makes you feel as if it were sucking out your brain. I try to make the sound. Maybe it's more like sreep, sreep. Once I noticed it, I didn't think I'd ever be able to ride the metro again, but then I realized that it had always been that noisy, it just had never bothered me before. Isn't that interesting? How something that had been so trivial before could suddenly start to bother you. Sometimes I really miss it, Andi says. The metro? Budapest. And the Balaton. Almádi. The Danube shore, the houses, the chestnut trees. And yes, the metro too. The feeling of walking down Andrássy Avenue. I almost say, look around, there are waves, palm trees, colorful tiles, pastel de nata, but I know this doesn't help. That's how it is. Here's the Balaton, there's the ocean. Wait a second. I sit up and dig around in my bag. What are you looking for? Close your eyes. I know she'll be very happy, but she won't hug me. Even though it's that kind of situation. Here we are on the coast, the stars above us, and she gets two of her favorite kind of chestnuts. But Andi isn't the sentimental type. When she realizes what I've put in her hand, she doesn't hug me, but she does rest her head on my shoulder for a bit. Andi, I've never told anyone this, but I've been doing cocaine for four months.

She would have never thought that. She asks me why I never told her. I answer that I didn't want her to worry. Or to talk me out of it. And do you want me to do that now? I don't want you to worry. You want me to talk you out of it? Silence. All Andi says, and in a calm voice, is: I don't think you left Péter to start doing cocaine. I would like to quit. And Márk? He's been sober for ten days. Supposedly that hasn't happened in two years, and it's because of me. Or it's partly because of me. He once told me he'd fallen a little in love with me, but it was a charged situation, I tried to handle it in the moment. He called me a couple weeks ago, told me he missed me and that I should come over. It wasn't clear whether or not he had some at his place. The worst part was when I got there and saw that there wasn't anything racked on the table. You know what I felt? Disappointment. I was in an exceptionally bad mood. Then later, he took it out of his bag, and I was relieved. I wasn't only relieved, I got really excited. It flashed through my mind that this wasn't right, but I ignored it. I was waiting for everything to be as good as it had been at the beginning, but instead I jumped into questioning him about the other women he's seeing. I kept trying to pull the details out of him, with whom and how much, how good was it, that it was best with me, wasn't it, and then I said I loved him. It was terrible. And what did he say? What should he have said? He escaped. I listen to the waves. Did you know that there are so many more species living in the ocean than on land, I say to break the silence. For example, there are some that light up the space in front of them, and that's how they communicate with each other. With light signals. Like lightsabers. Do you miss him, Andi asks. I would love to say I don't miss it at all, but that's probably not true. The comedowns were terrible, but the rest of it, of feeling infinite, of feeling no pain, that was pretty nice, I finally answer. I meant Márk, she says. For a while I say nothing. Márk is the same as cocaine.

What do you think will happen now? What do you mean? With you. I don't know. I think I should get divorced. I will get divorced, I quickly correct myself. Or I am getting divorced. And Iván? The usual. He pops up, then disappears, then pops up, then disappears. I mean, so do I. And he was even offended that I canceled on him several times. I was mad at him. It turns out, he even cheated on me. Last year. Absurd, no? In one sense it isn't at all, because as you know, these things happen, and this is exactly how they happen. I cheat on my wife with my lover, and I cheat on my lover with another woman. When was that, Andi asks. After I said I wouldn't leave Péter. We actually broke up. But still. I thought he was just as in love as I was. But now I understand that God can get bored with just about anything. There are patterns, and there isn't much room for deviation. And who was it? That's the best part. It was some former coworker who looked just like Judit. A Jewish woman with big breasts and a big butt. The one difference is that she had blond hair, and Judit's is black. I don't understand how I fit into the picture. I don't have big breasts, nor a big butt, nor am I Jewish. I didn't tell Iván I knew. I don't want him to explain, although it would also be bad if he didn't. He senses something is off, because last time he asked did you get it in your head that you'd be a dick to me? One day he called me to rant about Judit. It's as if she's not even there, as if she doesn't care about any of it, she doesn't give a damn about our family, all she does is work. She whines, that's how he said it, she whines about not seeing the kids, but then she'll drop everything to go to yoga or just about anywhere else, as long as it's not home. He said this to me, you understand, to me, who got this exact same thing from Péter. I told him that I also work a lot, that I'm not with the kids all that much, and while I could spend more time with them, I still need time to myself. And then he said, that's different. It's not different. It's the same. I actually think Judit might have someone else. I even asked Iván about it, and he said it's impossible. Because Judit isn't like that. I told him I'm not like that either. He thought about it, and then shut it down with how if she did have someone, it wouldn't interest him. But I'm not mad at him anymore. He should be happy, I hope everyone is happy. Péter too, and Márk, and Iván. I don't need to worry about men anymore, my dear Andi. All right, then, my dear Vera, then what are you going to worry about?

Sometimes I feel like I don't know anything about life, like I'm just learning the basics. I feel like I fucked up. That besides two kids, I have nothing, I am nothing, I've disappeared. You understand? I'm only present when I'm a mother, and I'm not even very good at that. And yet, last week, they told me to bring in toothpaste and soap, and I brought it in the next day. I even remembered Fruit Day. I was proud of myself. And then on Friday they came home and asked me why I never make palacsinta. Every mom makes it except me. Ten palacsinta. I don't know why it's so difficult for me.

There's work. I'm not saying I hate it, but it doesn't

interest me much. I'm not myself. Why don't I paint, she asks, to which I answer, I can't with both the kids and work. And anyways, I add, the three of us live in a twenty square meter room. Why don't we move into my mother's old office, I could have my studio in the attic. To which I say, it's full of my father's and grandmother's things. To which she says, why don't I clean it up. I start with, that's an insane amount of work. Her: there are companies that will do it for you. Me: but that's a lot of money, and honestly, I'm sick of the whole thing, I can't stand living with my father, I want independence, to not have to constantly live up to someone's expectations, to be told how I should raise my kids or hear about what I buy and for how much. Get a lease, to which I say, I can't do that by myself, to which she answers, ask for help.

It's insanely frustrating that no matter what I say, she already has three solutions, and none of them seem unreasonable or hastily slapped together. She suggests organizations that I could turn to, contacts of people she knows. She doesn't let me suffer or feel sorry for myself, instead she just talks about my life as if none of it is difficult. It's always been that way. The summer my grandmother died, we went camping together. We were looking at postcards by the beach, and I started to cry because I no longer had anyone to write to. At times like this, a person just wants a hug or some sympathy. But Andi: send her a postcard! But she's dead, I answered. It doesn't matter. Writing to her will make you feel better. I didn't want to feel better, I simply wanted five minutes to remember her and feel sorry for myself. In the end, I did write her a postcard, and then every year, if Andi was with me when I delivered the postcards, I asked her to sign them too.

I close my eyes. Someone is singing in the distance, some kind of Portuguese hit, Andi also starts to hum along. There's a large group, they keep singing louder and louder, they dance, hold each other's hands, strip until they're naked, and their bodies glow like white skeletons. I hope they aren't going into the water, I say to Andi, but she isn't paying attention. She's singing. Tell them they're going to drown. Andi smiles, c'est la vie, it's dark, everything is black, I keep swimming, taking breaths at three so my neck doesn't get stiff, little grains of sand are rubbing against my thighs, the water and the sky are touching, they melt into each other, I don't know if I'm swimming or flying, breathe out, pull, one, two, three, turn to the side, breathe, maybe next year I'll even swim across the Balaton. Vera, are you okay? I'm startled. They didn't go in to swim, did they? Who? All those people that were singing. I was singing. So I was dreaming? Are you okay? To be honest, I think I'm afraid, I answer. Of what? I want to say of death, but instead I answer: that I'll never be able to draw again. Why do you think that? The last time I sat down, I knew what I wanted to do, I had the subject, the composition, the colors, and all that bullshit, and I thought that it would all be okay. In fact, I was sure of it. It didn't turn out well. It was flat. Mediocre, generic. I saw something in my head, but what I drew was boring in comparison. Static. Dry. It was like the next second wouldn't come, like I'd become stuck in some cramped state. There was no calm. I look at it, and all I see is stiffness and limitation. Andi hums, purses her lips, gives very slight nods. Are you still talking about drawing? I let that go. What if this is all I'll ever become? Are you saying that you used to be talented, and now you aren't anymore? Yes. It's done, over. I get why you're scared, she says. But if you don't try, it won't get better. Maybe something else could help. A different technique or genre. Go back to animation, she says, and she takes out the pistachios that we haggled for at the market. Well, really, she haggled for them, I just stood beside her and smiled. The whole industry has changed, I'd basically have to start from zero. I don't know the new software, and I'd need a better computer. Right now the ocean is not only peaceful and majestic, it's also indifferent. It doesn't care at all what goes on with us humans. Andi's about to say that's just an excuse, I could ask my father to loan me money for a new computer, I could reach out to my old contacts, I could ask for help with the software, I could take classes. I understand, she says. Obviously she doesn't, but whatever. I guess it really isn't easy. It really isn't, I answer. Of course I could solve the problem, but I'm scared of the whole thing.

And what's going on with Péter, she asks. We spoke a few days ago, and I didn't want to complain to him in particular, but he seemed so normal, so understanding. It just slipped out of my mouth how hard it is to find my place at work and deal with the kids alone. And you know what he said? Reap what you sow. His tone changed immediately. It was scary. I was shaking from nerves. I'm afraid to file for a divorce for that reason too. What if all hell breaks loose? Sometimes I think I despise him. Even though lately he has been trying. Did I tell you about the gift he gave me? Andi shakes her head. He'd originally meant to give it to me on my birthday, but he couldn't wait. It was like an enchanted object from a fairy tale. Imagine a box, or no, a chest. You can open it several different ways, and each time you see something different. There are old photos inside, and drawings, little carved sculptures, and if you press a button, a young girl jumps, swims, hikes. I've never seen anything like it. I don't even know what to compare it to. Wonderful. He gave it to me, and I thought, dear God, where was this man the whole time? Why did he disappear? And then afterward, where am I? What's become of us? You remember who I was when we got married. A cheerful, pretty woman. You're still very pretty, she says, but I don't react. I was sure that we'd grow old together. I had a vision. I was waiting for the 4/6 at Jászai Mari Square, looking toward Buda, and it was dark, the streetlamps were glowing. I saw the tram, and then an image flashed in front of me. We're chatting in a room, we're old, and everything is cheerful. Maybe it wasn't a vision, but no matter what it was, it seemed real. It wasn't just a desire or something I imagined. Why did I bring this up? You were sure you would grow old together. Yes, but what was before that? What became of you two. What became of us. I don't know, two unhappy, disheveled people. Who look for happiness elsewhere. You know what I feel? Anger. Sometimes I imagine myself jumping up and kicking him in the stomach with both my feet, or beating his head against the concrete. And then I ask myself, who are you really angry at? Who do you want to kick senseless on the ground? I look closer and see that it's myself. The question is, how did I accept this? And why didn't I realize it? That's the worst thing. The feeling when I think of the person I became beside him. A nervous, pale-faced woman. Who has no self-confidence, who doesn't even know what she wants from life. I'm exaggerating on purpose, but you understand what I mean. I despise that person. And you know what? He does the exact same thing, he sits somewhere and despises me because of the person I made him. An aggressive, frustrated man, full of bitterness. We brought out the worst in each other. We dragged each other down into a cold swamp.

I start crying, even though I'd been trying to hold it in. Sand gets in my eyes, and it's like I'm crying sand.

Andi hugs me. She doesn't say it, but I know she's thinking to herself, it's okay, Vera. Everything is going to be all right. The worst part is that nothing good comes to mind anymore. Was there anything to begin with? I feel like everything was terrible, our life, our love, our marriage, the sex, all of it was a lie.

Did you hear what I said, she asks me, and she squeezes my arm. What did you say? That there were good things, that he was the love of your life. It's not true that it was all a lie. The sex? I remember you didn't used to talk about anything besides how much you'd climaxed. You said, Péter is like a prince. You were a beautiful couple, everyone loved you guys. You hitchhiked halfway across the world together, do you know how jealous I was of you two? That you guys went for it without any money because Péter was bold and resourceful. One time we went down to the Balaton. The guys were all helpless, and then Péter came, went out for wood, made a fire, and cooked the meat. You know what you said to me? Andi, what I love about Péter is that if there were ever an apocalypse, I'd survive. No matter what it is, a flood, a wildfire, the ice age, I'd survive anything with him. Remember how he took care of you when you were sick? I remember. He did a much better job than I did. I'd get irritated if he was sick. And if the kids were sick. I can't stand being patient at times like that. The whole it'll be all right sweetheart, take your medicine, and we'll drain your little nose with the neti pot, oh, you don't want that? Well, then we'll drain teddy's nose first, and then yours. He never had a problem with that. The last time they came home, they wanted to pretend to be zookeepers. I said, okay, I'll be the tiger, and I thought, they lie down and sleep all day like me. And then of course came the really, it's always fun to play with Dad. The last time the older one threw up, I thought it was in her head, and the next day she was perfectly fine, but whatever, she won't go to school, so I thought I'd bring her to work, and you know what she said? Mom, you're a lot nicer at work, and you smile a lot more. So you understand, they see me as a mother who's always tired, who they can't laugh or joke with. And they're right. Their dad is funny and cool. Cool, that's the word they used. And I can't even remember his sense of humor. Well, Andi says in a high-pitched voice. I don't think his humor was ever earth shattering, but he could be very charming with company, very relaxed and open. You never even liked him. I didn't like how he treated you. But it's true, we had a lot of fun together. Do you remember when we joined the EU, and we sat on top of the underpass and spoke jibberish all night? It was so stupid, but we laughed so much. Tell me the story, I say. I sit up, pull my legs to my chest and rest my chin against my knees, and I listen to Andi while she tells me about the man I once loved.

X. Péter, I came to tell you that I filed for a divorce. Vera, please. If I'm no longer important to you as a man, then let me be as a person. I'm not doing well. My results came back, they weren't good. They still don't know what the problem is. Think of me too, don't be selfish. I lean back on the couch, then forward, then back again, I play with my hair, I shake my head. It's extremely difficult. I really do feel selfish, I say to the psychologist. She's a tall blond woman with bangs that hang down over her eyes. Andi recommended her, two of her friends have seen her. I feel like he really could have some kind of serious disease. And why do we have to get divorced right away? I could wait a few years, and then he might ask for one. Vera, if you were to ask me about his illness, I'd say he's bluffing. You've already seen this before. Regarding the divorce, you've been talking for weeks now about how you don't see any chance to start over, and that you don't want to live in this state of uncertainty for years. I can see that you've thought over your decision carefully. And based on what you've said about your husband, I would guess that he might try to change your mind by manipulating you emotionally. That's what we're trying to prepare for right now. I wonder if it irritates her that her bangs hang over her eyes. I would love to go over there and push them to one side. It bothers me that I can't see her eyes. Can we start over?

Péter, listen. I have something important to say to you. Vera, look at you, you're so beautiful! I've been thinking about you a lot lately, and I realized that I really have done a lot of stupid things. I'm asking you to give me another chance. I'm sure we can fix this. Think about the example it would set for our kids. I start laughing. I'm sorry, I just remembered that Péter would have absolutely said kiddos, or our little darlings, with that much passion. How did you feel when you first heard those lines, the psychologist asks. I was annoyed that he wouldn't let me get a word in. Why didn't you say something? I didn't want to interrupt him. But he was interrupting you. Don't stand for it next time. Can we start over?

Péter, hi! Hi, Vera! You look gorgeous. Thanks. How are the little ones? I miss them so much. Péter, I wanted to see you because, and she interrupts, we could go to the zoo, the little chicks would love it. I almost laugh at little chicks, but in the end I succeed in saying it. Péter, please, listen. Of course, of course, but one second. You wouldn't believe it, but I got my results back. I'm silent. The psychologist raises her eyebrows. I'm sure she's waiting for me to stand up for myself. I thought I might wait to hear the results, I explain. Don't wait, stick to what you were going to say. Okay, I answer. Let's continue. You wouldn't believe it, I already got my results back. Péter, please, don't interrupt me. You interrupted me, she says. I falter. Don't react, don't try to explain. Péter, I filed for a divorce. The psychologist nods, I'm doing well so far. You can't do that, she says. Vera, do you not have a heart? You want to abandon a sick person. I don't know how you'd deal with the guilt on your conscience if I were to die. How am I supposed to react to that, I ask. Last time he threatened to jump out the window. You don't have to say anything. He's a grown man, *he* is responsible for his life and death. And you're a grown woman. You can choose to get a divorce. What are you really afraid of, Vera? That hell breaks loose. He told me I'd be sorry if I filed the papers. And what did he mean by that? Would he prove that I wasn't fit to raise my children? Would he take them away? Would he kill me?

Sometimes I think it's really simple. We started something when we were young, and it was good. We did it together, and it was good. Then we changed. Both of us, but not in the same way. Me this way, him that way.

And then it wasn't good. What could we do? We could divorce, amicably. But what if I'm looking at it the wrong way? That this all happened because I cheated? Look, cheating doesn't mean the relationship is automatically going to end. You could have realized the marriage was worth saving. Instead you realized the opposite. You said, and here she stops, she puts on her glasses, flips through the red folder where she keeps her notes. Here it is, she says, and she clicks her tongue. You said, and this is how you phrased it, that Iván was a catalyst in your life. She looks at me. I don't want to justify what I did. I made a mistake. I don't regret Iván, I regret cheating on Péter. I didn't think I'd be like that. I should have been strong, but instead I threw myself into another man's bed. It irritates me that I'm trying to sound so formal, I could say it a different way, but it's almost like I'm afraid of the words. It wasn't even his bed, it was Andi's. She gave me the keys when she went back to Portugal. My mom was looking after the kids, and Péter was at a conference. Why couldn't I say no? I was like a drug addict. We're not always strong. But I was strong at one point, I answer. I thought that if I could do it once, it would always be that way. Maybe I thought too much of myself? She finally fixes her bangs, now I can actually see her eyes. Do you want to tell me the story, she asks. What story? About when you were strong.

Before the wedding, Andi organized a bachelorette

party at Cha-Cha-Cha in the Kálvin Square underpass. It wasn't really a bachelorette party, I didn't have to answer a bunch of stupid questions, we just partied. Andi invited a few of our former classmates, and Iván ended up coming. We danced all night. Around three in the morning, Iván said he'd walk me home, but I said I'd rather stay at his place. We lay down next to each other and cuddled. This is a test, I thought. If I could resist the temptation, the marriage could begin. And really. Nothing happened. I was proud, determined. Now, thinking back, I can't be sure that it all depended on me. But it doesn't even matter, whatever happened, I still failed to be strong this time. Maybe it was a mistake, maybe it wasn't, she interrupts. Either way, we can make mistakes. We can forgive. Ourselves, just like we do other people. I let out a long sigh. So, just like I made mistakes and can be forgiven, he also made mistakes and he can be forgiven, is that it? Yes, of course, you can forgive Péter too. But you don't have to accept verbal abuse. You don't have to accept physical aggression. We're quiet. Thoughts are weaving in and out of my head. Whoever does it twice will do it a third time. And whoever lets someone hurt them will get hurt? And that means me?

Do I play the victim? I ask. No, absolutely not. Péter distorted your self-image, because he was the most important person in your life, and the trauma is still fresh. But think about it, you weren't a victim in any of your earlier relationships. You spent several years at home with the kids. No matter how we look at it, that's a vulnerable position to be in. And Péter used that. Not with bad intentions. It was an example that he followed.

I came to tell you that I filed for a divorce. We're sitting in Szimpla, in the gallery, it's pouring outside. Don't do this, Péter says. Every part of him is familiar, his forehead, his gaze, the way he holds his mouth. I could draw him whenever, how the lines curve from his neck to his shoulder, the veins on the backs of his hands. I didn't want you to get the court notice unprepared. I wrote that our marriage has permanently and irreparably fallen apart, and that the decision is uncontested. I'm sure it will be difficult, but it's still faster and easier than a unilateral divorce. That can drag on for a long time. We'd have to bring in witnesses, and I don't think anyone wants that. He stares at me. Uncontested, unilateral, look at all these words you've picked up, he says. His voice and his expression are mocking. You're unbelievable, that you'd do this. The only thing I asked of you was to wait. I waited. I'm not waiting anymore, I answer. It feels good to be unwavering, and maybe he's surprised too, because he doesn't say anything. It's just ten minutes of discomfort, focus on that, Andi wrote before I left. Ten minutes. At least he isn't bringing up his health, or the kids. You only think about yourself, he says. That's what you are. From his perspective, he's right. Or he's wrong. Is it worth bickering about who's right or wrong in a divorce? It's always about you. Those words aren't true, they can't be true. Not the always, not the only. Those words mean you think more about yourself than you should. That means you think more about yourself than I'd want you to, than what's good for me. I watch the bubbles rising in my glass, try to hold back my anxious smile. It really could be irritating. You're talking about something serious, and the other person is just smiling. It would bother me too. What are you smiling about? I'm already scared that you'll raise our kids this liberally, he adds with spite. Don't explain, don't ask questions, he can say anything, nothing will have any influence. If I made the wrong choice, I'll deal with the consequences, but for now I have to stand up and say, Péter, I'm leaving.

## XI.

Failure, that's the word I wake up with. I'd thought that if I filed the papers, I would be relieved. The sun is shining through the thin slits in the blinds. Tulip chest, old photos, cuckoo clock. It's hot, as if fall will never come. It cools down in the evening, but during the day, we sunbathe in our swimsuits. This isn't normal, my mother says. And yet everyone's here in the village.

Our Father, who art in heaven, hallowed be thy name. I read that on the plate hung above the doorframe. Five plates, with a line on each one. Thy kingdom come, thy will be done. There's a flower motif along the perimeter of the plates, either in red or blue. On earth as it is in heaven. That one has a grain of wheat draping over the flowers. Give us this day our daily bread. That one doesn't have any wheat, but since it's already shown up once, I would have painted it, as it is bread after all. And lead us not into temptation, but deliver us from evil. I look at the one before it. They left out a line. Forgive us our trespasses, as we forgive those who trespass against us. Did it fall off and break and was just never replaced? It seems more like they never put it up, there's no space on the wall for another plate. The bed I'm sleeping in belonged to Kornélia Knotelin and Ilona Sándor. Their names have been carefully painted on the headboard. Why were two women sleeping next to each other? Were they a lesbian couple? Or a mother and her daughter? Their house is full of ceramics, the daughter must have painted decorative plates. Mom, I can't fit all the plates. Which one should I leave out? Leave out the one about forgiveness. I've had enough, I don't want to forgive that idiot, Ilona might have said.

You need walnut trees, meat soup, and swimming, my mother said to me a few days ago. You can work later, when you're better. I didn't argue. She looks after the kids, my only task is to rest. She found a two-hundred-year-old peasant house. There's an enormous walnut tree in the middle of the courtyard, and a covered pool in the backyard. It's not very big, but it's an endless pool, so you can still swim in it. I didn't want to tell her that I had no desire to swim, nor eat.

I flex my right foot, flex my left. I don't want to do this, but I feel a strange compulsion to do it over and over again. As if only my feet existed, and they said: flex. It doesn't matter if I try to resist, the feeling comes back. Tingly. Like when I was a kid and had to step on the cracks in the concrete. I didn't have to, but if I didn't step on them, I'd get that feeling of temptation. It was important that I step on the crack with the center of my heel. If I couldn't land my foot perfectly, it was worse than if I'd never stepped on it at all.

My mother is being irritatingly jovial and positive. I think she just wants to show me that life is beautiful. She fried palacsinta, cooked corn, and made bean soup, and now she's skinning peaches. I know she'd give anything just to order a pizza, but she thinks this will make me feel better.

Today is my birthday. I look at my phone, I've already gotten a lot of happy-birthday wishes. As usual, my father was first, one minute after midnight, then Andi at 7:30 a.m. My great-aunt, the twins, my mother's second husband, my father's former coworker, my mother's friend and her daughter, the father of my elementary school classmate. Márk isn't among them. After I got back from Lisbon, I wrote a message in which I brought an end to the last few months. Of course, he brought an end to things by disappearing, but I didn't want to secretly hope, so I decided to message him. It was important that it not be too sentimental, but it shouldn't be dry either, nor should it be elevated or unnecessarily romantic, maybe sappy, it should have humor, but it shouldn't be irritating, nor shallow, nor light. I spent the whole day writing it, and while it didn't fit this criteria at all, I sent it. He wrote back, thanked me, said he'd be sure to answer. Or would definitely answer, I don't remember which words he used. I've been waiting since.

I hear voices from the kitchen. My mother mixes the peach with túró cheese, milk, and half a packet of vanilla sugar, with some cocoa powder on top. The kids are begging for seconds. No more. We have to leave some for your mother. But Mom doesn't eat because she's happy with the smells. She really doesn't eat, the little one repeats. My mother might be looking at the clock, she pulls them in closer. She doesn't have an appetite right now, she tells them quietly, but maybe she'll want it later. And the palacsinta? That's also your mother's. She's not even going to eat it.

I stretch my legs, tighten my calves. Ankle, foot, knee, thigh, right, left, right, left, thigh, knee, calf, elbow, armpit, right three times, left twice, I need to stop. I can't. I flex both elbows together again. Now I stretch the muscles in my chest, again the elbows, thighs, hips, butt, right, left, knees again, I do it faster and faster, I can't stop.

I think Dad would be a better mom than Mom is, the older one says. Her voice comes from the courtyard, they must be sitting around the table, probably preparing my birthday gift. Why do you think that, my mother asks.

Because he likes to cook and he mends our clothes. Mom doesn't like to cook, and she doesn't even know how to sew. And that makes someone a good mother? Yes. Not that she loves you both, that she takes care of you and looks after you? I don't hear what they say in response. And don't forget, your mother draws beautiful pictures. Other mothers can't do that so well. Mom doesn't draw because she doesn't have time. But she tells you such interesting stories. She doesn't tell us stories anymore. She's always tired. But she often sings to you. I imagine they're making faces, because my mother chides them. I don't want to hear that your mother's songs aren't good enough for you!

Ever since I filed for the divorce, it's been like this. My mother thinks I shouldn't let Péter see them. I don't want to be the kind of divorced woman who doesn't let her ex see his children, I answered. I turn onto my stomach, but the feeling doesn't go away, I still get the compulsion to move my legs, then my entire body. I turn over. I try to take a deep breath, but my lungs only fill halfway. I hold it in, count to five, in the meantime I'm not allowed to move anything. One, two, three, four, I tighten the muscles in my right leg. I feel like throwing up. What if this never goes away?

My mother doesn't give up, she tells the children in detail how good a mother I am, how much I love them, going on about all the things I do for them. I'm grateful for her. Dad's family is good because they didn't get divorced, the older one says, and Mom's tired. Mom's always tired, the little one mimics. Dad isn't tired. He even washed our sweaters. That's very good of him, my mother answers. Dads also have to do the laundry and clean up, we aren't living in the last century. Mom didn't wash our sweaters, and they were dirty. But Dad washed them. First he took pictures. He took pictures, my mother asks. My stomach clenches. Yes, he took pictures. And why did he take pictures? Is this leaf pretty? Will you tell me why Dad took pictures of the sweaters? So he could show it to the jury. I'm shaking. The jury? Yes, so he can show the jury that Mom's bad. Because she didn't wash the sweaters. Dad took pictures of them and then he washed them.

I close my eyes, lie motionless, concentrate on my breaths, the exhale is twice as long as the inhale, Andi might have said something like that once. Four in, eight out. Or was it the other way? It's most important to relax. I imagine breaking a vase over his head. I kick him in the stomach, rip out his hair, scream in his ear.

I dig my nails into my palms as deep as they can go.

My mom goes for a walk with the kids. I sit on the pool deck chair. It's a light metal structure with threaded plastic upholstery. You either sit at a right angle or lie down. Neither is comfortable. I should center it, make sure it's balanced, find the right spot. It shouldn't be too far forward or too far back, uniformity, that's what I'm longing for. It doesn't work, I'm constantly rocking forward or backward. I shouldn't care. Just relax. It works, but then comes the feeling that I need to move my legs. Slight flex on the right, and I lie back. Chest muscles, elbow, knee, foot, left, right. What if this never ends? The young woman gave up on continuously moving her body and collapsed in the backyard. Maybe they wouldn't write young anymore. V. Vera, Budapest resident. Middle-aged woman. How long am I still considered young? Restless leg syndrome. That's its name, although it's not just my legs. My entire body is restless. Supposedly there are two remedies, exercise and a stress-free life. I could try exercise.

I go into the pool. The water surges toward me, I lie on my back and claw at the waves. I hit the ladder. I need to claw harder to stay in one place. I try again, I've got the rhythm, I swim with my legs at an even tempo. If I help with my arms, I get a little closer to the surging water. Stick your stomach out, let your swimsuit dry, that's how they taught us. Hold your head straight. If I can put a can on your head, it shouldn't fall off. No matter if it's called backstroke, we're never really on our backs. Our torso is constantly moving. Arms and shoulders high, up at your ears, your pinkie touches the water first. Backstroke is easy. It's easier than freestyle, because you don't have to mess with your breathing. That's why I like it.

If I'm at the pool, I know when I'm getting close to the wall. Sometimes I even count the strokes so I don't accidentally hit my hand. Here, I don't have to count, all that matters is the even tempo. If I use more strength, my head will hit the tube that creates the current. If I slow down, my feet will hit the ladder. I have the right rhythm, the pace of my arms helps, the clawing is relaxed. I stare at the sky. It irritates me that I can't move forward. To that, my mother says at least I can perfect my technique. I don't have to worry about anything but my movements. But I want to move forward, watch how the ground moves.

My mom comes back with the kids, they sing happy birthday, I get two autumn paintings. We play Uno and listen to the radio, Eighties' Best Hits. I'm going to lie down, I tell my mother, and she strokes my head. I lie down in the dark room. I'm sure my father would have yelled at me by now, I need to pull myself together and go out to be with the kids. Why is my mother so patient? She probably wants nothing more than for me to get better. My father wants that too, in his own way. I need to move out. Look at apartments, get back to the city, live on my own.

I look at my messages, and Márk hasn't written. I don't know if I miss him or the cocaine. Or if I'm angry that he didn't fall in love with me. Iván hasn't written either, even though half our high school class already sent their birthday wishes. I did, however, get messages from our old neighbor, from my college classmates, my coworkers, Andi's high school classmates, and, out of her three brothers, the one who fell in love with a girl because she swung on the swings in a sexy way. Even from Terike. I believe that our Good Lord has blessed your relationship forever, and that He has planned a joyful future for you both after this time of hardship. I pray with hope and perseverance for your soul's healing, that you overcome the media's disease. The final victory is with the eternal, all-powerful God. Péter hasn't written. He used to make a cake every year until this one, maybe that's what I miss. It's strange that I don't miss anything else. His touch, his thoughts, nothing. I don't miss his mind.

Iván calls, and I wait for him to wish me a happy birthday. His tone is anxious. You're right, Judit has someone else. Is she in love with him? I don't know, he answers. I thought that was what was going on. So what's next? She said she'd break it off. That she'd stay with me, with us, with the family. But I can't believe her. She always has her fucking phone in her hand. I think she thinks I'm an idiot. You understand? She's constantly fucking around on her phone, she never goes anywhere without it. I'm already imagining the worst. Hair, smells, phone, chat, email, everything. I haven't slept for days, I've lost ten kilos, and I can't stop shaking from nerves. I don't know why he's telling me all this, or why I'm even listening. I don't even know how to react. I'm sure he didn't call so I could rub it in his face, so I could say what did you expect, or that I understand Judit, I know exactly how she feels. Love is like a drug, it's hard to get off it, I say rather verbosely, to which he answers, I understand everything, I'm just so fucking sick of all of it. I'm all insane jealousy, I despise myself. These are the sort of things he says. And that he can't stand it, he's starting to lose his mind. I can't feel sorry for him, I even tell him sorry, I can't feel bad for you. I'm being hypocritical, coming at him with how he should pull himself together and stop bitching about this. Look how much stronger I've become. Especially now that I've learned all the details about Péter. I pause for effect, then add, and about you. That you cheated on me too, not just on Judit. Don't say anything. Today is my birthday, anyway. Yes, he'd had that in mind.

Again, I hear voices from the kitchen. Who's going to help me beat the eggs? What are we having for lunch? Mom's favorite. She's not even going to eat it. She'll eat this, you'll see. Now pour some flour into it. That's enough, enough, enough! It's fine, you're doing a great job. Now, my dears, let's see what comes out of this. My mother has come out of her shell. It goes without saying that she hates cooking. I need a cutting board with a handle and a flat knife. You can take it out once the dumplings have come up to the top. We'll beat eight eggs. If your grandfather were here, he would have absolutely rolled his eyes and said, Babika, no more than six, ever, but remember, egg dumplings need a lot of eggs. They come in and grab my hand. Mom, you have to eat some of this, we made it. A dotted tablecloth, a large bowl of pickled cabbage. I sit facing my mother, who serves me very little. I eat all of it, my mother serves more, and I try not to cry.

My mother's former colleague wrote, as well as her current colleague, my father's childhood friend, two fathers and five mothers from the kindergarten, Andi's parents. And Márk's little brother, Gergő. He really loves the Chopin piece I posted, to which I say, it fits my melancholic spirits, to which he says, do I still draw. He always thought I'd turn out to be an artist. I should write that I don't draw anymore, because of the two kids, and anyways, the three of us live in a twenty square meter room, and also, I'm getting a divorce, and in fact, I was doing cocaine with your brother for four months, but instead I answer that I just started a new piece. I haven't started anything, I haven't drawn a single line since I left Lisbon. Can he ask what it's about, or is that a secret? It's not a secret. Though it would have been simpler had I said it was one, because now I have to answer with something. Water, I write. I'm surprised by how obvious it is. The ocean, the Balaton, the pool. But why that in particular? I almost drowned in the Danube once, and the feeling of water surging around me has always stuck with me.

Saying that I almost drowned is a big exaggeration, but it's true that we fell in. I went kayaking with my parents. Or canoeing, I mix those two up. Before the regime change, we went to Rómaifürdő every Sunday. My grandparents were managing one of the boathouses. My grandfather would tidy up the boats while we played Ping-Pong, or sometimes we went into the water. My father always sat in the back and steered, but this time my mother was doing it. I don't know whose idea that was, maybe my father had said, Babika, today you're steering. What I am certain of is that things could have gone differently so that we didn't fall into the water. For example, if instead of saying, Babika, steer left, my father had said, steer toward the shore. Or if my father had explained how that's the left side, the other one is right. Of course, it's irritating when one's wife doesn't know which side is left, but everyone knows my mother has problems with right and left. In any case, it wasn't my mother's bad steering that made us flip over into the water. At least, that wasn't the direct cause, it was that my mother suggested they switch places, because she was of the mind that if my father was going to be so impatient with her, she didn't want to steer. And then still, it could have gone differently. For example, if they didn't both stand up, or if they'd crawled from one end of the boat to the other. There could have been other solutions, but my mother was already hurt, and my father was already humiliating her triumphantly, Babika, how do you not know which side is left? They stood up at the same time, the canoe flipped, and all three of us fell in. My eyes had been open, it was like I'd ended up at the centrifuge. The water was roaring, everything around me was brown. My mother rescued me, and my father swam after the canoe.

Gergő asks about the ocean. It's like a huge animal, I answer. I could hardly get in it, it sucked the sand out from under me, I couldn't swim, I could hardly even get out, the waves were tossing me, they threw me onto the shore, my swimsuit, my hair, and my mouth were full of sand, my knees and my elbows were scraped. With Gergő I'm not quite as detailed. He asks me what medium I'm working in. I'm in an experimental phase for the time being, I write, I'm just drawing in sketchbooks, so pen, pencil, whatever there is. I'm planning on making an animated film. As I describe it, I'm filled with a good feeling for the first time in a long while. Maybe if I say it, I won't turn back. The kids rail at me: I shouldn't be messing around with my phone, I should tell them a story.

What story should I tell, I ask them on the swing couch. The one about the seasons. Where did we leave off again? Spring was sad and didn't want to come out. Yes, Spring unfortunately never came, however, Summer burst forth, a beautiful, stately, and strapping young man. That means, I explain, that he had nice, chiseled muscles. Big biceps, toned legs. This is a bicep, I say, and I show them. He had an intelligent face and a mischievous smile. Like Dad? More like Apollo. Who's that? The Greek sun god. Like Brad Pitt, my mother interjects while reading in the neighboring pool deck chair. Who is he? He, my dear, if you ask me, is the real Greek sun god. And what is Autumn like? Autumn is a mother, I answer. Is she pretty? She has some shadows under her eyes and a few gray hairs. She gives off a lot of heat in the daytime, but by the evening she wears out. Good day, Handsome Summer! Autumn says to greet him on a hot late-August day. Good day, Sad Autumn! It's time, Handsome Summer. I'm afraid you must go. Oh, dear Autumn, can't I stay a bit longer? The people don't want me to leave. They're happy that they can swim in the Balaton. Nobody, however, is looking forward to your arrival. Handsome Summer, you're too scorching and searing. You're making everyone sweat. People can't dress normally, and their foreheads are gleaming with grease. They can't sleep because of the great heat, and they have to turn on that awful air-conditioning, which gives them terrible colds. Believe me, they are already looking forward to my arrival. Oh, kindest and most understanding Autumn, I know you're fond of me. Let me stay here. This Summer is really trying hard, my mother says from behind her book. Just give me one thing. Let me stay during the daytime. Handsome Summer, you know I can't do that. Everyone is allotted their own time. So it's true, Summer says, disdainfully and mockingly. You're selfish. You only think about yourself. You don't care about people's happiness. My mother turns toward the kids. You see, this isn't very nice of Summer. We call this emotional manipulation. Autumn isn't selfish at all, she just wants to stick to the rules. And what did Autumn do, the little one asks. The kids look at me. In the end, she felt sorry for Summer, and she said, all right, let it be as you wish. I will give you a little more time. Three weeks later, she came back. Hello, you comely, muscular man who did not want to hand over your place and whom I generously allowed to stay, she greeted him confidently. Hello, selfish, bag-eyed mother who is jealous and who gets upset at the sight of people cheerfully drinking wine spritzers on terraces, slurping on juicy watermelons, chewing on cooked corn, and springing into the Balaton's cool waters. You can insult me, Autumn says with a smile. It won't hurt. Your time is up, you must give up. My mother puts down her book, looks at me, and raises her eyebrows meaningfully. You really think that people like you? Summer asks. What is there even to like? Your depression, from which you just cry and wail for days, that ceaseless rain? Your constant complaints about how tired you are, which paint everything gray? Your unpredictable behavior? You give warmth during the day, but in the evening you cover the earth with frost. The poor kids put all their warm clothes on in the morning, and then in the evening they have to lug all of them home. Autumn didn't back down this time. You're talking to me about unpredictability? she asks with her arms crossed. You, who thunders so loud when you're angry that you twist up the trees, who pours icy rain on the ground and beats down the harvest? I look at you, and what do I see? Everywhere green, green, green. Tell me, do you not get bored? You can't even mix colors. Where are the pinks, the deep purples, the rust browns, the mauves, the crimsons, the bright yellows? Your stridence and your vigor are convincing, I won't argue that, but without the fall harvest, where would you get wine for spritzers? Handsome Summer, Autumn said peacefully, believe me, if you go, the people will long for you, and they'll be glad for your arrival. Let's part ways in peace and not say anything bad about the other. They embraced each other and said goodbye. That's how Autumn slowly came to greet us.

I look at my phone. On the post in which I passionately thanked everyone for thinking of me on my birthday, Márk gave a heart. In the comments, he writes happy belated birthday, I heart it, and all I write is thanks, which he likes, after which I write him a message. So, what happened? You finally decided to show yourself? He answers, sorry, I was right, he did run away, but I'm really a wonderful woman. Do you want to meet up? This is what I wanted to ask. Or I wanted him to ask. Neither of us asks anything.

I boil water and spend a long time choosing between flavors of tea, turn on the radio, then turn it back off. I look at my phone. Márk sent another message. It'd be nice if you came over. I start to sweat. But last time you told me you ran off because I was too much, I write, not understanding, so that he can write, yes, but I've since realized that you're the woman of my life. I'll quit cocaine, I just need you. Door, room, curtain, balcony, sex, depression. Márk, I'm not coming over to party, I answer. Then we won't party.

I'm sitting at the table. I don't know what to do, I take out my sketchbook and draw a few lines. I feel like there's no point to any of it, I'm drawing bad lines. How can you draw bad lines, Andi would ask. It's not coming together. Why do I want it to come together immediately? It'll come together later. For now I'm just drawing lines. Straight ones, curved ones, rough ones, I can darken them, cross over them, shade them in. I enjoy how the pencil scratches on the paper, how it leaves a mark. I made the right choice not going to Márk's, I'm sure of it. I made the right choice, I repeat aloud. I couldn't have done otherwise, for myself, for the kids.

Gergő writes: how is it coming along with the ocean. It's not, I answer, I'm just collecting material. Have I seen *Spirited Away*? It's one of my favorites. He was just asking because water is important in that too. We chat about Japanese films, Hokusai's waves, and why I'm getting a divorce. I ask him why he broke up with the woman he'd been with for so many years. Seriously, you dumped her because she went corporate? He answers: it's a crime to not do what you have a talent for.

I sketch the interior of a room, I try to draw myself, how I'm sitting at the table with the lamp illuminating my hand. Rhythm, repetition, leaving things out. Lines that I draw through, lines that I thicken, that I draw carefully, nervously, long and short, unexpected shapes. It feels good to be surprised. Is this also me?

XII. I dreamed that I loved him. Strange, that it was on this exact day. We're holding hands, flying above Moscow Square, and like in my vision at Nyugati Station, I sense that we'll grow old together. Moscow Square. I'll become like my father, who still calls Blaha the EMKE. I look at my phone again. Twenty minutes. I take out the papers, sip on my tea. Cinnamon and plum. I'm already sick of winter.

Transcript of hearing open to the public. Petitioner, colon, that's me. Defendant, that's him. The case's subject, colon, marriage dissolution and allowances. Location of proceedings, time. Those who are present, a list, judge, the petitioner's lawyer in person, the petitioner in person, the defendant in person. After the opening of the hearing, the judge finds that the persons summoned have appeared in accordance with the summons. The presiding judge informs both parties that the hearing's content will be recorded via sound recording, and the transcript will be available for viewing at the judge's office within eight business days, while a copy of the transcript may be provided upon the payment of a stamp. The presiding judge makes known the petitioner's request, along with the written documents that have been collected prior to this date. To the presiding judge's inquiry, the petitioner's representative: I uphold the form of order sought by the petitioner. The petitioner maintains their unified declaration of intent in regard to the request of marriage dissolution. The petitioner has not yet reached a settlement with the defendant regarding allowances. The hearing's parties have moved out of their last joint lease and are no longer in possession of a shared dwelling. To the presiding judge's inquiry, the defendant in person: I don't request our marriage's dissolution. In fact, I oppose it.

Subsequently, the presiding judge informs the petitioner's representative that in hearing the defendant's declaration, marriage dissolution based on the parties' unified declaration of intent is not possible at this time. Thus, the petitioner must attach to the existing documents a detailed statement of facts regarding the circumstances of the marriage's failure within fifteen days. The petitioner must also attach documentary evidence and requests for evidence, and a definitive request stating the case on which the Court will rule. Thereafter, the

Court determined, and the presiding judge announced the following conclusion: the Court will delay the day's proceedings. New date of summons, colon, and here's where today's date shows up. The petitioner's representative requests the transcript by email. Hearing concluded, transcript closed at 12:30 p.m.

On the sheet's upper right-hand corner, I write first hearing, then slide it into the folder. The tea is lukewarm. I drink it quickly, then take out another sheet of paper.

We respectfully inform you that the application has been submitted according to the following facts: the defendant the petitioner, for about a year, more or less frequently, the petitioner was in love, the defendant was however, they both felt that since October, as a result they moved in together, Izabella Street, which was the last shared, on that day the petitioner and the defendant married, in the presence of the district's registrar, the petitioner attended university, part time, in an animation studio, creative activity, continued to create art, an eight-hour workday until September, the defendant at a multinational company, the parties' first child was born on this day, the defendant already, their second child, born on this day, the petitioner stayed home with the children, however, according to the petitioner the parties' relationship, of course the parties had disagreements, only that, this was first thanks to the petitioner feeling that it was better not to argue, thought that after marriage a woman's place was in the kitchen, at that time the defendant, spent evenings elsewhere, the defendant would often, late at night, more and more frequently, emotional distancing, for every small matter the defendant, nothing was ever good, into depression, the petitioner even suggested, or the two in couples therapy, asked the defendant if he was in love, the defendant answered, and for two or three years had already grown cold toward the petitioner, the relationship between the parties became worse and worse, verbally aggressive, cruel, bad tempered with the petitioner, and eventually, and that ended with, the defendant then pressed the petitioner's face against the bed, was afraid, became determined to, first there were arguments, the action was repeated, defendant, nothing happened, he threatened, lest, in summary, in our opinion the parties' marriage progressively, defendant, that the petitioner's role, wife and mother, should limit, took the statement of opinion poorly.

I need to leave, I just skim over the last page. In face of the petitioner's claims, according to which I physically abused her, I resolutely state that I never abused her. All I write in the top right corner is: Péter.

My stomach is tied up in knots, and it feels like my lungs have become narrower. The third gate at the entrance, sword, book, scale. With sabers out, we fight for the truth, but let us not forget that we are not the only ones with the truth. The lawyer said that too. You know, Vera, everyone who comes to me is convinced that they are right. Nobody has ever stood before me saying they're wrong. There are bright brass lions at the gate, they'll tear me to shreds. I glance over my shoulder, there's no one behind me. You aren't going to rip me apart, I think, and I pat their heads. I step into the lobby and falter, there's a crowd. I can't go in any farther. How are there so many people, I ask the bearded man standing in front of me. Supposedly it's some kind of extra screening. I've been coming here for years, he continues, and this has never happened before. Although, if we're to be exact, I've been here once, two years ago. Behind me a tall woman in a green coat takes out a sleeve of biscuits. Regardless of the noise in the background, I can't hear anything but the rattling plastic. Why don't those two doors work, I ask the bearded man. That's for the staff. He points to the one on the right. And that's the exit. See, it's written right there. He's helpful, not condescending, but I still take it the wrong way. Chewing, crunching, the woman behind me gorges herself ceaselessly. Her face is pale and sunken, and there are huge shadows under her eyes, like an enormous grasshopper's. Are you here for the first time, the bearded man asks. The typical chatterer standing in line, soon he'll be telling me his life story. I need to de-escalate. All I say is: no. His eyes are uncomfortably blue, his smile is double sided. I should tell him that I'm not that big of an idiot. I came with the lawyer last time and didn't pay attention to the doors. Divorce? I nod. I chew my lip, tear away the hardened skin with my teeth. The woman in the green coat is constantly devouring, munching, slurping, it's like someone is scraping my brain with a chisel. Excuse me, did you see the sign? It says you can't eat here, I say. She turns around. Please, finish your gorging! Mind your own business. I grab the sleeve and sprinkle the biscuits across the floor, here, eat them! If she were to bend down, I'd kick her. Instead I say nothing. I turn to the man. This is the second hearing. My husband doesn't want to divorce. I have to prove that the marriage really did fall apart. I have to describe everything that happened in detail, call in witnesses. I don't want this. I thought we could divorce peacefully, that there could be a mutual agreement. I talk without stopping, and the man listens quietly. I'm sure he thinks I'm another typical chatterer standing in line.

There's a sign next to me. In the interest of securing the life, physical wellness, personal freedom, and personal property in this building, cameras have been placed on the premises, which will be recording motion pictures. What a convoluted expression. It is forbidden to bring weapons, with the exception of weapons used for service, into the building, including tools for stabbing or cutting, throwing stars, and staffs connected by chains or other bendable material. There's a name for that in Japanese, but I can't remember it, ninjaku, or something like that. Andi would know. In addition to those listed, it is forbidden to bring switchblades, slingshots, pepper spray, replicas of weapons, tasers, rubber batons, and handcuffs. What's a throwing star, I ask the bearded man. You know, it's a small flat kind of weapon, the star's ends are flat and pointy. You usually throw it like a frisbee, that's how it got its name. It's not deadly per se, but it can still cause a lot of discomfort, he says with a smile. In my head, I knock out all the tall woman's teeth with a throwing star. But don't forget, says the bearded man, raising his index finger, blessed are the meek, for they will inherit the earth. He almost winks. I'm unsettled by it. I look at my phone.

There are men in uniform at the entrance. Let's close the door, one of them yells. Let's go, come up here, please. They say everything in plural. Maybe they think it sounds more polite. Good morning. Put your phone there. He points to the gray plastic bin on the black conveyor belt. Just like in Fátima, only smaller, and you don't put wax body parts into them. Anything in your pockets? Yes, keys. Keys, great, then put those in here too. Please step through. A metal detector. It doesn't beep, but there's a problem with my bag, they pull me aside. A blond curly-haired boy is standing at the counter, Mihály, I read on his name tag. There's something feminine about him. His cheekbones or his delicately curved mouth. Wallet, workplace key card, a crumpled-up Kleenex, a glasses case. What are we looking for, I ask in plural, maybe so that I seem more polite. Just show me your bag. A notebook, tampon, lipstick, pen, hand lotion, lip balm, the inside of a Kinder egg, a pink hair tie. That's my daughter's, I say. Put them on the table, please. But these are just personal things. The blond boy doesn't answer, he just drums his fingers against the tabletop. Deodorant, a folder, inside the court summons and the transcript of the first hearing. My bag is empty. This isn't good, Veronika. I do a double take. Nobody calls me Veronika. Nobody. How do you know my name? He takes a five-pointed throwing star out of my bag. That's not mine. I didn't even know those existed until just now. But when you heard about them, you immediately wanted to test it out on the woman standing behind you, didn't you? I feel myself turning pale, I'm shaking. And here's another thing. In his hands are two staffs connected by a chain. In case you forgot what they're called, they're nunchaku. I don't know how they ended up on me. You wanted to strangle your husband with these. This is some kind of misunderstanding. I didn't want to kill anyone. But you thought about it. That's not true! Be careful what you say, Veronika. He leans forward and whispers in my ear. Remember. It was just a stray thought, I stammer, a vague idea, it wasn't serious. I read it on the sign, staffs connected by chains, and for a second, I imagined how much simpler it would be to kill someone with one of these rather than with your bare hands. Yes, I imagined it was in my hand, but I swear, I didn't want to kill anyone. Not even my husband. Prove it! How? Eat it! He puts the staff in my hand. I'm sorry? Put it in your mouth, chew it, and swallow it. You're joking. Did you not hear what he said, says the tall woman standing behind me. Eat it! I want to run away, but the woman grabs me. I yell, nobody pays attention. I look around, and in the courtroom, grasshoppers with human faces are chewing. The woman in the green coat shoves my head into the purse, there are thickly woven webs everywhere. Reap what you sow. Hot steam burns my face. I start crying. Blessed are those who weep, for they will be comforted. The blond boy's voice. Now, there you are, ma'am. That was the culprit. A dumpy man is holding a jar of lens cleaner. You're very pale, ma'am. Are you all right? The woman in the green coat and the blond are nowhere to be found.

I'm standing in front of the paternoster lift, nobody's coming up, nobody's going down, the lift cabins are moving in front of me at an even pace. I read the sign. Please use the revolving passenger train at your own risk! Is everything all right? asks a familiar voice. The bearded man from the line. I didn't know they called it a revolving passenger train, I say, and point to the sign. And do you know why they call it a paternoster? I remember it has something to do with a rosary. Pater noster, qui es in cælis, Sanctificetur nomen tuum, he recites, and his voice echoes in the empty space. You know the whole thing? My grandmother was a Latin teacher. I know *The Odyssey* by heart, he says. I only know "Boci, boci" backward. The melody too. Does it interest you? You have no idea. Klim emos dnif nac ew erehw evil ot gniog era ew liat on srae on woc delkcerf, delkcerf, I sing. Impressive, says the man. It doesn't seem like he's mocking me. Have you ever tried riding this all the way around? He nods to the lift. Never. You won't try it now? Is it safe? I ask. What do you mean? You know the horror stories about how it'll flip you over and grind you up if you don't get out in time, I explain. That can happen, the man answers. I wait for him to start laughing, or at least wink, but his face is motionless. But that's not true, I say. You think so? I want to spit back of course I do, but I can't move my mouth, it's as if someone sewed it shut from the inside. Go on, try it. And don't forget, blessed are the pure in heart, for they shall see God. I take a step toward the lift. The cabin descends slowly. And if I'm not pure of heart, I ask. The bottom of the cabin is almost even with the floor. I look at the man, his blue eyes are glowing. Then it will flip you over and grind you up headfirst, he says with a loud laugh. Ma'am, you can wait until the day of judgment, but it's not going to start moving. It's the dumpy man, from security. It's written right there, don't you see it? There it is, right there, in red. Due to a mechanical failure the lift is out of service. I couldn't have put it in a more obvious place. It was working before, I say. Ma'am, this thing hasn't moved up or down in three days. This is the fourth time it's broken down since September. But the gentleman saw it too. I turn around. There was a bearded gentleman right there. Look, ma'am, I haven't seen any bearded gentlemen, but you've just been standing here like a little lost orphan. I don't understand, I stammer. You don't get it, you don't get it, you have to walk, there's the stairs, right there. You're young, a few stairs won't hurt, will they?

I go up to the second floor and look for a bathroom, I feel like I'm about to throw up. Loud retching, only a little saliva comes up. Blessed are those who vomit before a court hearing, for they will be relieved. There's no one in the hall, I go over to one of the courtrooms. Hearing notes. Call number, time, case number, case category. Uncontested marriage dissolution. Case related to Caseo insurance, parking surtax. I sit on one of the benches. Everything is quiet. I take out my phone, then put it back. I don't have patience for anything. I stand up. I look at the sign again. Auth. invst. into custody allowances. The auth., I assume, is authorities. Seven letters spared. Investigation, eight letters spared. Is it written somewhere how and when you should abbreviate things? Uncont. mari.

dissol. Twelve letters spared. Ágnes Szabó Szallayné, Géza Szallay. Blessed are those whose divorce is uncontested, for their past love does not go undeserved. The clacking of shoes, the rustling of coats, the rattling of keys. In their black robes and their black tights, with their large bundles of papers, the judge women stride down the hall.

My stomach hurts, I tell the lawyer. I can't stand this, my stomach is heaving. Don't worry, he can't hurt you. You're sitting by the wall, and I'm right next to you. Arrange yourself so that you can't see your husband. I'm sure he'll rock in his seat, stretch out his neck, just like last time. He'll hiss, sigh, groan, don't pay him any mind. Always look at the judge when he's answering. And if his lawyer asks a question? Look at the judge then too. If she speaks, don't interrupt her, don't whisper anything. Here's a pen, take notes. You can clarify afterward.

I sit next to the wall. I'm shaking, my teeth are chattering. Please stand. Tell me why your marriage has fallen apart. Even my voice is shaking, I speak slowly, with few words. What I say isn't enough. I need to express everything more elaborately. I need to say words. For example, cocksucking whore. I need to say sentences. I should sew your mouth shut. I need to explain actions. I'm hanging clothes to dry, he's standing behind me, he trips me. A joke. That was just a joke. I'm washing up in the kitchen, he strikes my face with a dish towel. He throws a chair at me in the living room. I need to answer the lawyer's questions. No, it didn't hit me. Yes, out of anger. Yes, it was clearly aimed at me. Yes, I stepped back. I don't know. I still don't know if it would have hit me had I not stepped backward. He kicked me off the bed and stuffed my face into a pillow. Finally, you're crying. What happened after that? Please, continue, I'm listening. What happened after that? He said, if you keep provoking me, you might make a killer out of me. I asked him to move out for a short time so that it wouldn't happen, so that it wouldn't happen, I repeat it like a broken record, so that it wouldn't happen. So that what wouldn't happen? The irreversible. Something irreversible. So that nothing irreversible would happen. I lean against the table. Please, continue. At first, he agreed. He'd take some vacation days and go to the countryside. He didn't go. I'm sick with a fever. You want to put a sick person with a fever out of their own house? I told him this wouldn't be any good, that it wouldn't end well, but he just kept putting it off, said you don't have any right to kick me out of my own apartment. I asked him to leave. He didn't. He stayed. He didn't want to go. Please, continue. What happened afterward. Would you tell me what happened afterward? He had to look at something on the laptop. He opened it up. I was still logged in. He laughed, ha ha, here are all your emails. I asked him to log out. To log out of my email account. He opened one of my emails and read it aloud. He was mocking it. Please, stop! He wouldn't stop. Stop! I wanted to take the laptop out of his hands. He wouldn't let me. He twisted my phone out of my hand. He twisted it, put it in his back pocket. His expression was crazed. Like when he locked me out on the courtyard balcony. I panicked. I didn't have my phone. I couldn't call for help. I wanted to get it back. My phone. I wanted to get my phone back. I yelled. What did you yell? I don't remember. I think I said give it back. He didn't. He put the laptop down on the bed. Or rather, he threw it down. Or he chucked it. He put it down forcefully. Can you show me how? Thank you, continue, please. He grabbed me with both hands. He pushed me down. He knelt over me. You mean he knelt on you? Not on me, over me. Where was his knee? His knee? Yes, where was his knee? Somewhere next to me, off to the side, and he was leaning over me. Let's clarify, so, the defendant's knees were beside you, one on either side, and that's how he was leaning over you? I think so. You don't remember? I remember him yelling, how can you humiliate me like this? How can you humiliate me like this. His thumb was on my neck. Both of them? Both of them. He squeezed it. He squeezed my neck. Will you show me where he squeezed you? Thank you, please, continue. What happened after that? He let me go.

Thank you, you may sit down. With the help of her notes, her memory, and her own words, the judge repeats my statement. She records it, later someone will type it up, and I'll read it in a PDF. In American movies there's always someone sitting in the courtroom, typing furiously. I listen to the judge, there's no stumbling, no repetitions, everything is succinct, as if it wasn't me who said it. She asks if I have any comments to add. None, Your Honor. And the defendant? Yes, there are. Péter stands up. Your Honor, I've been misrepresented. I would like to resolutely deny, in any case, that I harmed my wife physically. I've never harmed her physically. I don't understand what she's talking about. I look at the judge. Does she believe me or Péter? On what basis does she believe anyone? She must have seen so many of these cases before. He hit me, I didn't hit her, he said this, I didn't say that. Does she watch our words or our gestures? Does she look for giveaways? Who knows where the truth is. If someone were to play the scenes before us, would we still see it the way I said it?

I'm lying on the bed, his two thumbs are on my neck. What do I do? What do I do with my legs? Do I kick at him? My hand. Do I try to remove his hand from my neck? Do I yell? Why don't I remember? How long did it last? One minute, half a minute, only a few seconds? He suddenly let me go. Why did he let me go? He jumped up from the bed. What is he doing? Why are you hurting Mom? The little one's voice. How did she get into the room?

Where was she before this? The kitchen? Her room? I'm not hurting your mother, she's hurting me. Your mother is cruel, you see how cruel she is? Stay with your father, it's what's good for you. What do I do? I stretch out my hand. I stretch out my hand, but the little one pulls back. She cowers into Péter. No, no, unfortunately no, right, my little one? We don't need Mom. Mom is crazy. I'm standing in front of the bookshelf, the couch is behind me, Péter in front of me. I can't bring myself to take the little one from his hands, I don't want us to tug on her, me under her armpits, Péter at her legs, like in some movie. Péter's expression is crazed, and I'm sure mine is too. I'm calling the police. That's what I threaten him with. He doesn't react. How did I get my phone back? Did he give it back? Did I take it from him? Did it fall out of his pocket? Give her to me, or I'll call the police. I'm sure I said this. He hands the kicking child over to me. Does he hand her over to me this easily? Was it enough that I threatened him? Did he take it seriously? Was he scared? Or did he just want to leave? The little one's crying, she doesn't want to be with me, I set her down, Péter gets dressed. I follow him. I'm divorcing you, I tell him. My voice doesn't shake.

Right now it's in fashion to claim domestic abuse. I think, in fact I'm convinced, that my wife has been taught what to say. I would like to go in order. I never said we should get divorced, that I absolutely deny. It's true, one time I said I didn't love her anymore, but I was just trying to see how she'd react. The line that she could make a murderer out of me. I find it laughable that she still quotes that, that it made her that scared. I understood the sentence to mean that if she kept provoking me, and let's not mince words here, I was very much provoked, enough that I would have given her a nice big slap, and thank God I didn't do it, therefore, if she continues to provoke me, I could go into a state in which I am a danger to myself. That's how I understood it, and not any other way. That she wasn't interested in housework, that's a fact. Clothes were left soaking for weeks, food was rotting in the fridge. Nor did she deal with the kids as a mother should do. How do I put it? Yes, I think that a husband has a right to this. And of course the sort of crude things the petitioner has stated have never come out of my mouth. Was I sometimes a little irritable? Yes, that's true. And I asked for forgiveness. If I had to, I'd ask right now too. If she'd look at me. But she won't look at me. And, Your Honor, this sort of behavior has been characteristic of my wife all throughout the last few years. She let go of my hand and left me to myself, she wasn't interested in any of my hardships. I lean forward so I can see him. He has a piece of paper in his right hand, and he's gesticulating wildly with his left. We're past our turbulent period. I not only had problems at work, I had health issues as well, and I haven't even processed my mother's death. My wife, however, is only interested in herself. One of her friends just got a divorce, they're constantly partying together. I told her to be careful, I said, Vera, these things are a slippery slope. My lawyer interrupts: if possible, could you ask the defendant not to deviate from the subject. To which he says, I would like for the jury to understand the full situation. Could you please stick to the point, the judge asks. Regarding the first act of violence, and that is the first supposed act of violence, I would like to note that my wife has not said a word about how she came home drunk in the company of another man, with whom she was carousing in the doorway of our building. All I asked her when she came upstairs was to go to the other room. I didn't kick her off the bed. There was no violence from my end. He sits down.

His lawyer stands up. Your Honor, I would like to point out that the second act of violence suggested in the petitioner's claims is completely infeasible. From my perspective, it is absolutely clear that the one committing an act of physical violence was the petitioner herself. She wanted to grab the laptop out of my client's hands, and she kicked him in the back. It is also completely infeasible that, after such an event, the petitioner would not try to obtain a doctor's note. And there is no doctor's note. And I can explain this with just one thing. That what the petitioner claims did not happen. Does the petitioner have any comments to add? I stand. Yes, Your Honor. I would like to note that I did not jump onto the defendant's back. I sit down. The lawyer looks at me, nods. I'm sure he's surprised that I was so resolute. But what if I'm wrong? What if I really had jumped on his back? Why would I have jumped on him? Why wouldn't I have? Does the lawyer have any more questions? Yes, Your Honor. I would like to ask the petitioner why she did not try to obtain a doctor's note. Please, stand up. I stand up. Please, answer the lawyer's question.

Péter opens the door, outside the snow is coming down. I'm divorcing you, I tell him. My voice doesn't shake. He turns around. Don't you even dare report this, because you'll regret it. Nobody's going to believe you. You're crazy, nothing happened. You hear? His expression isn't crazed, it isn't anxious, he's confident. Nothing happened, you're crazy, he repeats. I'm standing in front of the mirror, looking at my neck. It's not bleeding, there's just a bluish splotch. Could it be that I'm actually crazy, that nothing happened? My neck is red. It's red because he grabbed it. He didn't just grab it, he squeezed it. He didn't just squeeze it, he strangled me. It hurt. I was scared he would kill me. That's why I yelled. I yelled so loud that my throat hurt. I'm not crazy.

Your Honor, I start. Now that this is happening, it's very clear what I should have done. But I was in a different state then. My husband threatened me, and said that no one would believe me. Also. I stop. I think about what word I should use. I also had a sort of shame. I just wanted calm and safety. I didn't think we'd get to this point, that this sort of thing would be necessary. Thank you, please sit down. The petitioner's answer to the defending representative's question in person: I can say that my husband threatened me, that he said no one would believe me. I'm also ashamed of myself. I didn't think we'd get this far, that this would be necessary. Do you have any additional comments? I would stand and correct myself, say I'm not ashamed of myself, I'm ashamed of the situation, but I don't stand, I wait for it to end. I pick at the skin on my thumb, I try to breathe evenly. I'm no longer shaking. Blessed are those who hunger and thirst for the truth, for they will be filled. The voice is familiar. I glance over, my lawyer has disappeared. Péter's chair is empty. His lawyer, the judge, are nowhere to be found. Is the hearing over? Was I supposed to leave, and I stayed here? Or did I come back? It's as if the room is smaller. I stand. The walls are moving, like in *Star Wars*. Being squashed flat isn't the prettiest way to die. 3PO, come in. 3PO? Shut down all the garbage mashers on the detention level, will ya? Shut down all the garbage mashers on the detention level! I rush out, the halls are empty. The paternoster is working again. My name is on the sign in red letters: Veronika, short order, go up to the fifth floor. I step into the lift, everything is quiet, all I hear is the machine's murmuring. A door opens facing the paternoster. My footsteps echo in the empty space. I enter the room. There are four people sitting behind the lectern. The blond boy, the bearded man, the woman in the green coat, and Father Lajos. Come closer, Veronika, says the blond boy. His shoulders are wide, his chest muscular. Before you ask, yes, we're the ones you're thinking of. And I wouldn't waste another word on that. Do you know why you're here? I think so, I answer. I'm glad, says the blond boy, and his voice is soft, though his expression is cold. I'm sure you know your name means the one who brings victory. I know, I answer. This kind of name is particularly useful in a court hearing, is it not? To have victory over the other party. The bearded man winks. But nobody calls you Veronika. Nobody, I answer. Everyone calls you Vera. Everyone, I answer. But I'm sure you're also aware of what the name Vera means. I'm aware, I answer. Lajos, would you please. Father Lajos takes out a piece of paper. Vera is a freestanding nickname of Veronika, in Slavic languages the name is independent and means faith. He raises his index finger and repeats: faith. All that Latin has to add is truth, the one who speaks truth, a teller of truth. I therefore believe, the blond boy says, we'd better stick with the name Vera. Please, we're listening.

I don't want to speak, I don't want to say words, sentences, which everyone here knows better than me. I close my eyes. Iván watches *Tom and Jerry*, Iván plays the intro from *Delta* on the piano, Iván asks to slow down while stroking my butt in eighth grade, Iván kisses me in Andi's kitchen, Iván and I are lying naked in Andi's parents' bedroom, Iván disappears, Iván introduces the sporty girl, I don't see Iván for years, but sometimes I write his name on the bathroom door while Péter waits in bed. Iván kisses me at the class reunion. Iván touches me in the phone booth. I'm pushing a baby stroller and thinking about how I came in the phone booth. I'm bathing the kids, imagining what it would be like for Iván to be inside me. Iván is inside me. Péter asks where are you and I lie that I'm with Andi.

We're waiting, Vera, says the woman in the green coat, and her voice is filled with warmth and trust. I now notice that there's gold trim all along her green coat. Father Lajos smiles. Only the blond has a cold gaze. The cold makes me shiver. I take a deep breath. Blessed are those who say the right words at the right time.

The blond stands, his expression does not soften. Come closer, Vera. Maybe I'll fall. They'll toss me into the deep. They'll strike me in the eyes with a throwing star, they'll tear me apart with the lions, they'll strangle me with nunchaku. The blond takes my hand. His touch is soft, his skin warm. Go. Where? He nods to the right, and I turn. I'd never noticed it before, but there's a paternoster here too. Where? Always up, he says. Don't get off. Will it grind me up? He doesn't answer. I step into the lift. Will it grind me up? Just go. Will it grind me up? Will it grind me up?

My lawyer gently kicks my ankle. I look at him. Answer, he whispers. I would appreciate if you could answer my earlier question, Péter's lawyer says. He seems on edge. I'm sorry, Your Honor, I didn't hear it. What was the question? Would the gentleman please repeat the question. Your Honor, I would like for it to go into the transcript that the petitioner ignored the question I asked three times, and now she claims to have not heard it. And now I will start over, for the fourth time. Will you refuse your husband custody of your children? I think over what the trap is. Is there a trap. If I refuse it, they'll pin me down with why didn't you ask for a restraining order. If I don't refuse it, what I've said thus far will become unreliable. Did you hear the question, or would you like for me to repeat it a fifth time? I heard you. Then will you do me the courtesy of answering? I will not refuse his custody. The lawyer continues. I understand, then you won't refuse. I'm very glad to hear it. However, that brings me to question. How is that possible? Understanding what you've claimed before, that the defendant, I quote, verbally and physically abused you, held you down on the bed, choked you. According to your testimony, the defendant is a violent man. So I don't understand, then, why would you not refuse him custody? There's silence. I look at the camera in the corner. I hadn't noticed it before. But do they always watch it in the security guard's room, or do they only take out the recordings when there's been a problem? The defendant attacked the petitioner, the petitioner attacked the defendant. Maybe the two lawyers went at each other. Will you answer my question? I look at the judge. All my husband's aggression was directed toward me. He was always calm around the children. They like being with him. I won't prevent them from seeing him. Thank you, Your Honor, I have no more questions. With that, this hearing is dismissed until a later date. When will it end, I ask the lawyer. Don't worry, ma'am. You'll get your divorce.

XIII. There's no snow, only cold. It could be that this year's winter will pass without snowmen or sledding. I'm standing in the room in front of a large mound of clothes with a blue shirt in my hand. I was wearing it on that day. The pants, a pair of black jeans, I've already thrown out long ago. I should throw this out too. One shouldn't bring their past with them. I don't want to throw it out, it's made from good material, good trim. Not every shade of blue looks good on me, but this one does. Is everything okay, my mother asks. I show her the shirt. Would it be weird if I wore it? Like I don't want to break away from the past, like I want to live through it again, stay a victim forever, that sort of thing. But if I threw it out, it would be like regressing. Or is that stupid? My mother thinks about it. The point is freedom, she says, and with that she grabs a suitcase and goes out into the entryway. I fold up the blue shirt and put it in a different suitcase. My mother is watching from the entryway, and I want to explain that if I was to throw it out, it wouldn't be an honest gesture, just a desperate attempt at something. I'm still not over it, and for a while I won't be. In the end I don't say anything. I don't think she was expecting an explanation.

We're leaving Buda. I'm going back downtown, back to Andrássy Avenue, the 4/6, dog shit. I won't have to take a taxi and wait a half hour for the bus. I'll miss the trees, but at least everything will be close. I think about the arrival, how we unpacked the car while the kids argued about who gets to sleep in what bed. Dinner, a bath, putting them to bed early. I'll have my own room, I can watch porn at night. Mom, tell us a story! Leave your mother alone, my father tells them. No calamity. Or at least no big calamity, and that's good. I can usually make decisions, recognize my mistakes, and if I need to, I can change. We often get to the kindergarten on time, and it's not always me who forgets Fruit Day. If I'm really drunk, I write Márk. He doesn't answer. The next day I'm ashamed, and I tell myself that this was the last time. I called Iván, asked if he wanted to meet up. I told him I got my own apartment. Judit is pregnant, he wants to be a good husband and father. I told him I was rooting for them, and that's true. Gergő writes sometimes, but lately I've been seeing a young woman in his pictures. Andi thinks it's time for me to get back out there. I have no desire to. Chat, meet, listen to divorced guys about how shitty their ex-wife was while they listen to me about how shitty my ex-husband was. My soon-to-be ex-husband. Andi advised me to write about the kind of man I want in as much detail as I can. She thinks that if I describe him, the universe will listen and send the right person, that's how she found her job. I don't believe that, but just to be safe, I wrote down what kind of man I would like, underline, colon, dash. In the IKEA bedding section, I brooded over whether I should buy a one- or two-person comforter. Two-person, Andi said immediately. It's a bold gesture, the universe will take it into account. I've decided that I'll have lots of plants. I got a peace lily from Andi, it's the least demanding, start with that. I can't overwater it or let it dry out. That's it. Maybe it'll work. Everything else too. It'll be easier to keep the bathroom clean. I can move around the furniture, and if something is really heavy, I can ask the neighbor for help. If the sink breaks, I'll call a plumber. If I don't call a plumber, we'll brush our teeth in the bathtub. I'll make spaghetti and meatballs. If I don't cook, we'll order pizza, or we'll go down to the gyro stand. It won't be an issue for the kids to eat two yogurts one after another. I'll draw every day. I'm no longer afraid that it'll turn out wrong. I'm afraid, but I don't care. I care, but I can brush it aside. I experiment.

Sometimes I feel like it's successful, and then my heart starts to pound.

Mom, tell us a story! We're sitting on the bed in the kids' room, I'm looking at the blank walls. If I look out the window, I see the neighboring house. I miss the trees. Everything is so barren. How will I know when spring comes? Mom, tell us a story. What kind of story? About when we were born. Once, on a nice day not too long ago, God cleared his throat. Line up, my little souls! It's time! I need someone who would like to be born in Hungary. A large group of souls stepped forward. Who among you, he asked, would gladly go to Budapest to be with a nice cool mother? Many stepped forward. And then he continued. The mother is ultimately kind, but sometimes she loses her patience, and then she yells. He didn't really say that, the little one interrupts. Why wouldn't he have said it? This is exactly what he said. He also added that the mother loves to sing old Hungarian pop songs, but her tone is a little off. And this narrowed the circle, many did indeed step back. And also, God continued, she doesn't like to cook at all, nor bake, so you will only get palacsinta in very limited amounts. And now, many of them did indeed step back, because most of the little souls had a sweet tooth. Now, there was still a large number standing in front of him, so he continued. She won't buy you every little plastic toy, and no matter how big of a fit you throw, you will only get cotton candy once a year. Nor will she be happy if you take her lipstick and do not put it back in its place. He didn't say that! Okay, maybe he didn't. The point is that in the end, there were only two little souls standing next to each other holding hands. Hmm, so it's just you two left, God said. Wonderful. So, now you need to choose who's going down to earth. We'll only go together, because we love each other so much. God looked down at his papers and frowned, not a chance, that would be too much for the mother. You must choose. But the two souls did not want to be separated from each other. And so he said, okey dokey, all right. God doesn't say okey dokey. You know, God isn't at all like we sometimes imagine him to be, I answer. Can he say things like okey dokey? Of course. And then he added, one of you goes first, and I promise that the other will follow soon after. The two little souls were glad. They hugged each other, and they cried a little over being separated. Then, God grabbed the hand of one of the souls. It's time, he said, and he started her on her journey to earth.

I look at the walls. They're big and blank, but at least a nice pretty white. The room smells like fresh paint. I let out a deep sigh. What's wrong, Mom? The walls are big. I'll put up your drawings, it's too empty like this. You don't like it? It's like on Izabella Street. Izabella Street. They no longer call that home.

XIV. I can't struggle. There's too much movement in struggling. Take the steps one by one, not too fast, but with power to it, your feet should be tapping softly on the concrete, focus on the movement, the size of the steps, breathe gently, in through your nose, out through your mouth, right leg forward, left leg forward, right, left, relax into your shoes, let your body get into it, glide, shoulders down, turn your palms inward so there's less resistance, just like you're swimming.

I move forward at an even rhythm.

© Péter Máté

**RITA HALÁSZ** is a Hungarian author, art historian, and teacher. *Deep Breath*, her debut novel, won the 2021 Margó Prize and was a finalist for the Libri Literary Prize.

**KRIS HERBERT**, who also goes by Kristen Herbert professionally, is a fiction writer and translator from the Chicagoland area. After living several years in Budapest, she completed an MFA in creative writing at the University of California, Riverside. She is a 2024–25 Fulbright grantee doing research on Hungarian crime literature at the University of Szeged. Her own work of crime literature is a long-coming work in progress.